The Dregs of Presque Isle

*Book One of
The Chandlerville Chronicles*

CHRISTOPHER CHAGNON

All rights reserved. All characters appearing in this work are fictitious. Any resemblance to real persons, living or dead is purely coincidental.

No part of this publication may be reproduced, distributed, or transmitted in any form or by any means, including photocopying, recording, or other electronic or mechanical methods, either now known or unknown, without the written permission of the publisher, except in the case of brief quotations embodied in critical reviews and certain other noncommercial uses permitted by copyright law. For permission requests, write to the publisher, "Attention: Permissions Coordinator", at the address below.

Grey Wolfe Publishing, LLC
PO Box 1088
Birmingham, Michigan 48009
www.GreyWolfePublishing.com

© 2013 Christopher Chagnon
Published by Grey Wolfe Publishing, LLC
www.GreyWolfePublishing.com
All Rights Reserved

ISBN 13: 978-1628-280005
Library of Congress Control Number: 9781628280005

The Dregs of Presque Isle

*Book One of
The Chandlerville Chronicles*

Christopher Chagnon

Dedication

In memory of Denis Chagnon, Willie Hanson and Craig Schwenn. This one's for "yous guys". "Decent!"

Acknowledgements

I would like to thank the folks of Onaway, Michigan for providing me with a place to grow up that was like no other. The pages that follow are some of the reasons why. Although this novel is fictional much of what you will read may have happened if you close your eyes and imagine.

I thank my wife, Nannette, and my children, Justine, Marcel and Luc, they have always been supportive and encouraging. Also, my friends, Rah Madden, Mel Perkins, Clark Chapman, John Perkins, and my brothers Glenn, Denis and Verdie, who have given me memories and fodder to write about. Thank you Dick Parker, you are man of few words but a vault of wealth with your command of the English language. There are more friends and acquaintances that are too numerous to put on this page but are certain to surface in some chapter further along in my writing career.

Finally, each of us has had someone who has made a mark on us, especially at an early age. Perhaps, they didn't know at the time, but I believe Bob Donia, my 12th grade English teacher did. Thanks, Bob, for instilling a dream in me in 1969 that has never left.

Prologue

    The narrow passage to the room was cold, damp, and frighteningly dark. But I made my way past the blue curtains that hung heavy from the ceiling in the dimly lit parlor, and through the twin doors. I was sneaking in to see Remy Fortier laid out on the porcelain table; pale white, stiff and dead.

    Two weeks earlier, we were climbing the tall blue spruce tree next to the Rectory after catechism, but polio killed him within a couple of weeks. At least that's what the death certificate stated. My father stood over him wearing a white lab coat, while clutching a cold, saber-like steel instrument in his gloveless hand. I was shocked at the sight of Remy. His lips were like dead rose pedals, and his skin was drained of color. He looked more like a mannequin in Fay's Clothing store than the boy I went to catechism with, and had to say five Hail Mary's, and five Our Fathers as punishment from the nuns for climbing the tree during mass. There were bruises covering his body that should have healed since we slid down the wide, pine needle boughs and crashed on the ground. Mine had.

"You might as well come in, Chris. I know you're d'ere. It's time," Pa was preparing to embalm Remy and unceremoniously introduce me to the funeral home business for the first time. I hesitated for a moment, sheepish, afraid, and then stepped into the embalming room. The air was pungent with a bitter smell of embalming fluid that burned my nostrils. A small fan tried to suck air outside with a slow churn through a portal in the wall. I hovered near, and clutched the paint chipped doorway as he walked with great indifference around the body like a hunter about to field dress a deer. He was a professional.

This was the first dead body I ever saw. I didn't cry as I watched my father work on Remy, even when he took the long saber looking trocar, and thrust it back and forth into the young, yielding skin of Remy's stomach to evacuate its contents as the grey white coat he wore floated away from his legs. The frightening sucking sound of the instrument pulled and ripped away at Remy with gushes of blood and debris until the clear, pink embalming fluid emerged, and drained along the trough of the table. "Venez ici," he said to me while motioning to come to the table. "Massage his arms to bring da blood up his body-like dis," He took one of Remy's arms firmly and pushed his skin upward. This brought a gush of thick blood through the cannula where it drained onto the porcelain table. I held his stiff arm and made a feeble attempt but couldn't do it so he did. When he was finished embalming he looked at me and said in his joual French Canadian dialect, "Beyah."

Mom stepped into the room and put a compassionate hand on my shoulder. "Romeo, he's too young for this right now. The other boys were much older when they started." she said.

"He came in and dat showed me he was ready. Why else would he come in? He did fine, Mildred," he replied.

"He went to school with this poor child, for heaven sake," she said, "I don't think…"

He interrupted, "Let's see if he comes back. Dat'll tell if he's too young," my father said as he removed his bloodied lab coat.

There were untimely deaths; Tommy Bloom died when his tractor tipped over and crushed him in his barnyard. Lucille Schmidt was killed when a car strayed off the road and struck her while she walked her dog along M-33. Horace Frank drowned when his canoe tipped over on Black River. Death was easy to find, and we saw it in all forms, shapes and ages. I was going to see more embalming on that frighteningly cold porcelain table in years to come. This was the way it was going to be for me, and my two older brothers, for the rest of our time living above the funeral home my father owned, the Romeo Cosette Funeral Home in Chandlerville, Michigan. The year was 1958, and I was eight years old.

Chapter 1
1963

Chandlerville's main street was dotted with a couple of smoky bars and the drab Midway Diner where country songs played out of a nickel jukebox and spilled onto the street. A clutch of muddy Chevy and Ford pick-ups and sedans lined the curbs. Patrons sat with disinterested stares, exchanged gossip, and drank countless cups of coffee poured by big bosomed Lila. The fiftyish waitress still hadn't found Mr. Right. Meanwhile, at the Leed grocery store, shoppers poured in and out throughout the day and evening. There was Swede's Clothing Store, the Five and Dime, and Stone's Theater, a two-story stone block post office, a Dairy Queen, Brown's Shoe Store and Fay's Clothing Store. In front of the gothic stone block courthouse stood a profound bronze statue of Emmitt

Chandler holding an axe in one hand and bible in the other. An inscription on the statue base read:

Emmitt Chandler, founding father and first resident of our fair city.

The Cosette Funeral Home, a tall and narrow thinly painted brick building sat beside Flynn's Pharmacy. The pharmacy and funeral home were close enough to pass notes from window to window. We lived above the funeral home. All of this was fine and normal looking to the short stay visitors who came and went in our fair city, but lurking in the backstreets, and in a place we called the Ruins were ominous and forebodingly evil forces at work. Forces of vile bigotry, unnatural deviance, and bold defiance lay submerged waiting to surface. Dogs and cats went missing, windows were broken, car tires were slashed and some old folks were fearful to leave their homes at night. No one could prove it out right because of the clandestine nature of the crimes, but most people believed it was the work of the Frenchtown Gang; Fred Millender, a tall, pug faced, big boned dolt with sloping shoulders who didn't have the sense to come out of the rain, Buckshot O'Toole, an acne pocked fifth-grade drop out with short stubby legs and thick torso resembling a troll.

Then there was Dave Manton, a slightly built, fleet fifteen-year old boy with jet-black wavy hair and gentle eyes who lived with his frail mother across the street from Millender. His older sister, Mary, drowned while swimming in the stone quarry ponds when she dove head first into a limestone shelf that was concealed in the dark green water. He was an enigma. Two years earlier he faithfully held the chalice of hosts as a humble altar boy at St. Paul's, but in a sudden transformation, shortly after his sister's death, he changed from a 'good' catholic boy to a Frenchtown menace. Father Klein took to Manton in a kindly way, and bestowed nice gifts and money on him, but something abrupt and sinister took hold of him like a mysterious unexplained illness. But Bill Pratt was the gang leader in no uncertain terms. Pratt's father,

Ivan, was a villainous character who crashed in and out of Bill's life like a November storm across Lake Huron. Ivan Pratt's residences included the County Jail and Jackson State Prison where he came and went like the seasons serving time for habitual offenses of assault, grand theft larceny and forgery. The apple had not fallen far from the Pratt family tree as young Bill was bent on following his father's footsteps. Ivan Pratt was cruel. Bill's forearms and chest were riddled with cigarette burns and scares from endless beatings he endured from his father. Ivan chopped the head off a chicken in young five-year old Bill's presence. The headless chicken ran frantically about in aimless circles and frightened the younger Pratt to tears. In a dreadful and cruel joke, Ivan Pratt took young Bill's head and placed it on the chopping block, raised the axe high above his head in a mock beheading, then laughed while violently shoving him to the ground.

Every blow he took and every burn he withstood were the ingredients that boiled in the caldron of Bill Pratt's rancid soul. There was no redemption in store for him, only a furious and venomous reaction to life. There was no other choice for him to make for someone else had determined his path.

Chapter 2
The Fort

    My brothers and I did things that we didn't want our parents to know about. A few blocks in any direction would take us out of town, and into the burnt blue sky and brown farmlands and forests of Presque Isle County. There was a toughness a kid had to have living in Chandlerville. Sometimes, painfully acquiring respect from each other by smoking cigarettes, fishing at the Kleberg Dam's concrete spillway when the floodgates were open with water gushing past in a tumultuous blast, or being able to make a meal out of what we could catch, clutch, club and kill. Diving off the Tower Pond trestle was nearly as much fun as the ride there when we 'borrowed' the D&M Railroad's hand trolley for an afternoon. My oldest brother, Verdie, concocted most of these precarious, and precocious activities. He was named after my Uncle Verdun, but we called him Verdie. He was sixteen years old and could run faster than any kid in town. He was starting to develop rock-hard biceps that rippled in taught bulges. Light brown hair that Mom described as 'dish water blond' capped his prodigiously creative mind, and he was not bound to any conservative restraints, especially if it was fun. Another impressive talent he possessed was his ability to draw and sketch. He could whip together wild and hilarious caricatures of anyone who caught his attention. Sometimes it got him in trouble, like the time he drew an unflattering rendering of Maude Miller, the spinster English teacher, sitting on a toilet reading a Mad Magazine.

My other older brother, Denis, was willing to go toe to toe with anyone that got in our way. He was tall with heavily muscled arms and legs that formed into a rather protruding, bulbous hind end that gave him extraordinary strength. His brown hair twisted in a waving cowlick in the center of his forehead, and he had a good singing voice, in fact, all three of us did. That is why Mom put us in the St. Paul's Church Choir. We sang harmonies to 'Frere Jacque', and 'The Rosebush and the Briar'. Occasionally, Pa assembled us at one of Chandlerville's three bars to perform, and he would collect gratuitous bottles of beers for the act. I hadn't developed any special talent yet, but Mom said it would come.

We found the wide-open country of northern Michigan, and the escapable little town of Chandlerville to our liking. Paragons in play everywhere we ventured, and trouble when we weren't looking for it. It was easily found around every stale corner of the bleak diminutive town of one thousand.

We were waiting for Froggy Fitzpatrick in the fort we had built in the fallow field between Fred Fromm's dry cleaners and the funeral home. Verdie reached into the vase that held a half-dozen Queen Ann's Lace stalks and pulled one out. He held it in his tight lips and struck a match to light the other end. He took a deep draw of smoke and coughed violently when the stalk flamed and shot a burning burst of smoke into his lungs. "Uhh...Damnit, I should have wet the end. I always forget to do that," he said coughing between words. Froggy flipped the burlap bag we used for a modest door to one side, and crawled in clutching a brown bag.

"Ay," He said in a gravelly voice. We 'ay'd' him back. Most of the fort's members were present now. There was Verdie, Denis, Craig Flynn, a red haired fifteen- year old who was as tough as a red head could be, and me. Craig's mom made him take piano lessons and they owned the drug store next door to our funeral home. His parents weren't always pleased that he spent most of his time with us. We had waited for Froggy in great anticipation; he had the smokes. Froggy Fitzpatrick's heavily freckled face displayed a white ring curling up his cheeks from the powdered doughnut he ate earlier, and he was dressed in bib overalls and a dingy white tee shirt stuffed behind them. He was Denis' age, fifteen. He had an uncanny ability to catch fish and spoke in a gravelly voice like Froggy from Spanky and Our Gang. Occasionally, he would try out for a spot in the school choir just to watch Mrs. McAtee wince at his hilarious inability to carry a tune with his comical voice.

This was our meeting place late afternoons after school, Saturday morning and most everyday throughout the summer. We worked hours by digging with broken shovels and dirty fingernails to hollow out a spot in the field of tall grass behind the funeral home. Dirt walls and a sod roof held up with wood planks kept us secure from inquisitive eyes and ears. Great plans were made within the comfortable confines of our fort. A moldy rug, a small wood burning stove, homemade bows and arrows, a couple of rickety wooden fold out chairs pilfered from the funeral home, and a couple rusty pails used for ad hock tables decorated the hideout's interior. We were comfortable as hell inside.

"Got the fags?" Denis asked.

"Old Golds from Shoemaker's," Froggy replied when asked what brand he stole.

"Decent!" I responded.

"What about the Winston's you promised?" Verdie asked.

"Old Bill had 'em too high in the rack and I couldn't reach."

"What the hell, no filters?" he shrugged. "I guess theez'll do," Verdie protested even though he just fried his lungs on a flaming stalk. Finally, we gave our approving, "Decent!" The expression of decent meant that everything was cool and totally acceptable but it had to be said in a peculiar throaty vernacular, "Dee cent!"

"Oh, Oh! Hear what Millender, Manton and Pratt did to Johnny?" Froggy blurted.

We all frowned, "Whaa?"

He grimaced and contorted his face into what looked like a baby eating mashed peas and said, "Made him eat dog shit! Yeah, imagine that, ay? Sonszabitches!"

"What?" We shuddered with gapping expressions of curled lips and stretched faces. William Perceval Pratt was his full name. Pratt hated his middle name and hated his father for saddling him with it. He went berserk at the mention of Perceval. Knowing this, the older teenagers around town called him 'Purse Evil' or 'Percy' with indignant disaffection causing Pratt to go into a fit of rage. The wayward boys lived down by the railroad tracks in shabby, black tarpapered shacks, near the granary on the north side of town. Everyone called this area Frenchtown. Gruff and grimy, green teeth, and mean as hell, the depraved Bill Pratt was well known for terrible acts of bullying, thievery, and malevolence. Pratt spent a lot of his time in reform school for stealing, joy riding a cop car, and an assault on Lloyd Levin, the town's meek chief of police. But many of his devious deeds went unpunished. Pratt was muscled and mean, but clever; he always managed to gain his release to return to Frenchtown and resume his wicked work.

"They'll get theirs," Verdie said as he carved a notch into a cattail shaft.

"How we gonna' do that? They're big bastards, Verdie. Pratt even tried to beat up his Dad," I said.

I never had to fight; and the truth be told; I didn't want to. I was always around the older boys and felt intimidated by their size and experience. Whenever there was trouble my older brothers always stepped in to save the day. Like the time Eddie Sloan was giving me some shit about looking at Carmen Portice who he had the 'hots' for. Sloan was a couple of years older than me and was jealous of anyone who looked her way. He grabbed me in the hallway by the English room ready to take a swing at me. Denis saw it coming down, and laid a heavy fist on Sloan's jaw. Denis stood over top of the crumbled Sloan and screamed, "Don't ever touch my brother!" Sloan never looked my way again.

"I'll figure something out. We got ta' be ready. It's just a matter of time before they start on us. We got to protect the fort, too...At all costs," Verdie said in a concerned tone. I picked up one of the many papier mâché flowerpots that were stacked in the corner, and began to cut eyeholes into it with anticipated urgency. Verdie saw that I was getting worked up and calmed me, "Not right now, Chris." We collected used flowerpots after funerals to use as head protectors. They were thickly molded papier mâché containers that resembled Roman helmets. A couple of holes to see through, and a piece of kite string under the chin, and we were ready for imaginary battles. The bases of the rectangular containers were filled with an inch of tar so they wouldn't leak when the flowers were watered. We stuck pages from the Detroit Free Press onto the tar to keep our hair from sticking. I continued fashioning my helmet and put it on for fit but I forgot the Detroit Free Press. Craig gave a swift smack with his wooden sword to the side of the helmet that made my ears ring.

"Perfect!" I said while I painfully removed the twisted flowerpot head protector from my tar imbedded hair. We always tested our mâché helmets with a couple of clangs before we put them in our stash. We felt invincible in our grey papier mâché Roman helmets.

Pratt's gang, however, used knives and fists to wreak havoc on their prey, and he was deadly accurate with a peashooter. For fun, he would hide behind a bush or car and pelt younger kids with his shooter and they never knew what hit them.

"Time to head down to Tuff's Pond for more cattails. We gotta get stocked up. Those Frenchtown pricks will be after all of us sooner or later. Let's be prepared," Verdie warned. "Remember what Troupe Master Thompson said?" There was a moment of collective silence, and in unison we shouted. "Be prepared!"

"Prepared? I thought he was sayin', be repaired," Froggy said through his nasally gravel like voice. This drew a couple of sharp pokes to his ribs, and a joint 'you gotta be kiddin' laughs. We had gone to one Boy Scout meeting but found that the troop's activities were too tame and boring. We didn't like following orders, either.

"Okay, let's get the bucket ready," Denis said, and reached for the rusty tin pail sitting on the ground. We gathered around the pail like pagans in a secret ceremony, unzipped our pants, and began urinating yellow streams into the bucket. Up the zippers went, and up the bucket went above the doorway on a precarious shelf. Anyone breaching the doorway would receive a good drenching of urine.

"Guys? Craig? Don't forget the bucket when we come back," I said being sure to remind Craig in particular who had forgotten about the bucket from time to time.

We started out to the pond, but first we would stop to pick up the dog shit eating Johnny Harkens. We couldn't wait to hear about it.

Chapter 3
The Boxing Lesson

    We darted down the back alley to Main Street. Past old Armand Leed who owned the only grocery store in town. He lived on the eastside of the alley to the funeral home in a white two-story home that was well kept. Along the front of his house was a wrought iron fence that had fleur-de-lis adornments that stuck out like spearheads. The white haired old man was mixing paint from leftover cans into one large one to paint his backyard fence. He wore a white panama jacket, and white trousers that were splattered with paint and grass stained knees. His white bushy eyebrows grew together across his wrinkled and tanned forehead. His youngest son, Bill ran the grocery store, and his oldest son, Bob, owned Fay's Clothing that sat adjoined to the grocery store, but Mr. Leed always knew what was on sale. Most of the time he was working on his house that sat perched castle- like above Main Street.

"Where you boys goin'? I got a job for yas," he said inviting us to paint his fence.

"Sorry. Mr. Leed, ar pa's sent us to yer store for some stuff," I quickly replied.

"Oh, well that's good. Bread's on sale four for a dollar And don't forget butter. Lowest price around," he barked and went back to mixing paint.

Booz Danker was coming toward us, staggering along the sidewalk in front of the Post Office. Booz was our town's drunk, and a punch-drunk ex-fighter. He liked us. He had made his way from his house on the hill past Tuffs Pond down to the local bars. He had no trouble making it downtown but after an afternoon in the Northland and Metropole bars his wobbly walk home was difficult. Characterized by his two steps forward, and one-step back gate, he was immediately recognizable from a distance. His bronze leathery face was riddled with scars from his days in the boxing ring, and he smiled when he saw us. He went into a fighter's pose shadow dancing around in a circle while thrusting his fists at his imaginary opponent. He cast a lethargic jab down low, and a follow through right cross that a blind man could dodge. We began to dance around him pretending to pummel our opponents like he was.

"That's it boys, hit 'em high, now low. Uh, uh, uh, step back and finish with a cross. Like this," He stopped his routine and bent down on one knee and counted to his imaginary foe, "One...two...eight! Yer out!" He burst out in a loud hoot and spread a broad grin showing a couple of yellow stumpy teeth in his purple mouth. "Lemme show yas' how ta' get a guy in a clinch an grind his eyes ta' swell em' up," I was standing nearest to him and he pulled me close to his chest. The smell of beer and sweat hung on his face like a stale bar towel. He held his left arm around the small of my back encircling my raised fists tightly to his chest. "Now tilt yer' head against mine like this." I felt the clamminess of his oily, white haired scalp press on my forehead as he pulled me firmly toward his head. Then I felt the sting of his boney skull grind into my eyebrow and I tried to pull away but couldn't. "Now givem' a couple a rabbit punches to hiz back," I felt a deeper sting in my kidneys when he lightly thumped my lower back with the inside of his fist. He released me and I pulled away shaken but unharmed. Our eyes lit up in awe from his lesson. "Lemme tell yous about my fyett with Coot Jeggs. Now thaa was a fyet," Booz recounted, but soon forgot what he was going to say. He always brought up Coot Jeggs, and the battle the two of them waged 15 years earlier in Saginaw. It was the last fight for either of them as they beat each other into a stupefied draw that ended their boxing careers. We left, and laughed and punched each other in the arm as we made our way toward Harkins' house. Booz, punching and swaying, staggering and laughing, made his way toward the Metropole.

We scurried past the verdant lawns on Main Street beneath a big-clouded sky and cluttered back alleys on our way to Harkins's. We got to Johnny's in time to watch him trying to retrieve a dime with a stick and a chunk of gum. He had dropped the coin between the house and the concrete steps. His brown-patched Beagle, Schenley, sat amused atop the porch while Johnny fished out the coin. "Get on theyah you little-got it," Johnny said in his Boston accent. The dime was probably going to buy his dinner that evening unless we made it to Moser's cheese factory or Tuff's Pond before dark. We plopped down on the cool concrete porch like kids in a classroom, and petted Schenley while we waited expectantly for Johnny's story.

"Let's hear it. We want to know what happened with you and the Frenchtown ass'," Verdie said.

"So you heard abat it, ay?" he said looking away with his lowered head, ashamed of his acquiescence. "Just headin' from

Fassbindah's turning in some tonic bauttles I flipped on him the day beforah. They caught me by the cheese factry. Manton held me down, and Millendah stuck a piece of Shenley's shit in my mouth. Pratt stood theyah givin' ohdahs."

"Did you have to swallow it?" I asked.

"No. I just held it theyah while they mashed my cheeks tagetha like this," he said while clamping his hands over his face. "I stahted to throw up and they stahted getting sick and pretty soon all of us wah throwing up like when one baby stahts cryin' and all the othah babies staht cryin'. Not Pratt, though. He had a shit eatin' grin on an' just laughed at us. It was kinda spongy like ..." Before he could continue we grabbed our guts and bent over in a mock vomiting posture. We cringed and set out for Tuff's Pond.

Flipping. That's what we called stealing from old Wilhelm 'Bill' Fassbinder, a bespectacled plump man in his 80's who owned a convenience store across the road from Tuffs Pond. Bill was a relic from WWI where he was on the Kaiser's side. He conducted an unscrupulous practice of tipping his weight scales in his favor and shortchanging people when they brought copper, lead and aluminum scraps in for salvage. We knew what he was up to so we tried to even the scales by flipping bottle returns and used batteries. We brought our returns to the store to get our less than correct return from Bill and one of us would come back the next day to retrieve the items from his back room and resell them to him. Sometimes he was wise to it but he could never remember who we were. Bill was partially blind, and he couldn't recognize us unless we told him. Johnny's older brother, Chubba and Bobby Precour, his buddy from Black Lake, would put on fake beards and wire rimmed glasses and buy beer. We hardly ever saw Chubba, and he didn't care much what happened to Johnny. Chubba wasn't his real name. It was Melvin. He got the name Chubba for obvious physical attributes. He was a good looking dark haired teen who had skinny birdlike legs that progressed to a slightly potted belly. He knew how to use his bright blue eyes and tempting smile that often made the girls blush. He was, forever, preoccupied in an endless sexual pursuit of Eunice Cummins, the young and dainty 11th grade Home Economics teacher. Chubba made it a habit to leave his manhood exposed in a longer than necessary display after draining his bladder. The Harkins family was quite dysfunctional, with their self-employed father trying to make a living cutting wood. The two boys and their sisters Kate, the youngest, and Kay the oldest who was always looking out for a new guy in town, were trying to keep them together in a losing battle. Mostly, the dutiful Kate filled in as mother but she was the youngest, and didn't have much leverage. Mrs. Harkins died years before when they lived in Boston.

Chapter 4
The Bloated Frog Race

Farnsworth McIntosh, 'Farny' as we called him, leaned against a street sign dragging on a cigarette waiting for his mother to pick him up in her Plymouth Cornet. His blonde, greasy hair was combed straight back on his head and jutted outward over his forehead like a waterfall. The hair on the back of his head was fashioned into a V that was called a 'd a', or duck's ass. He was trying to be cool and tough looking but his constant stutter and facial tics made it difficult for us to take him seriously. We got along well with Farny, despite his Frenchtown Gang attire; blue jean pant legs rolled into cuffs, a pack of Camels rolled tightly in his tee shirt sleeve, black points, and sulking strides with his head tilted to one side. This was how you looked tough in 1963. Farny knew the Frenchtown Gang but he was not of the same mean disposition. He lived outside of town with his mother, Beatrice, an aged spinster who had Farny by her one encounter with a man, a sailor home on leave eighteen years earlier. Behind the greaser appearance there was a softer side hiding beneath his smirk. He didn't have much use for Pratt and his gang. They steered clear of each other. Farny could handle himself in a fight and Pratt knew it.

"Farny, how they hangin'?" we joked.

"Long and….la..la..low," he replied with a stiff, jagged smile.

"Safe to go to Tuff's Pond?" Verdie asked.

"Haven't seen any assholes ta..ta til now," he said through a long exhale of smoke, and another grin.

We were a block away from the pond, and we could smell the pungent stench of stagnant water and cattails. The bog near Frenchtown had cattails, but Tuff's was more alluring and safer for us. We sloshed our way through the soggy trail we made by countless trips to its banks where a sprawling willow tree spread it's stringy arms down to the water's edge. Through the dense, interwoven swale grass, horsetail reeds and bulrushes, we trudged onward in ankle deep scum, disappearing like bees in a great hive, unseen by anyone far or near.

Tuff's Pond was a confluence of spring runoff from the Rainy River, and Stoney Creek. A wall of thick swale grass lined its edges in a nearly impenetrable barrier only to be breeched by young boys with the will to get to it knowing the pleasures that awaited. Large, beefy legged bullfrogs and slithering water snakes provided us with a day's fun with our handmade bows and arrows, and spears. Its perfect rectangle shape looked manmade, and probably was. By early summer it became a green, slimy, pollywog and mosquito-infested mire where only a trickle of water drained in and out of it. It was a target gallery full of frogs, snakes and turtles.

The sweat dripped from our red faces, and trickled down our backs soaking our shirts in a clammy, cotton armor.

Mosquitoes floated about our heads like dive-bombers as we vainly flailed at them. We marched on knowing that each clumsy step brought us closer to our aim.

"There's a good group of stalks over there, guys," Verdie shouted while catching his breath and pointing to a green, slender cattail cluster near the bank.

"Hand me the knife, I'll staht cuttin' 'em," Johnny said wiping his brow with his dirty forearm.

"Make sure you cut 'em all the way down at the bottom, and leave their fur tops on," Verdie instructed.

"I know, I know, geez," Johnny said while opening the foldout blade.

We gathered the perfectly straight shafts in a pile, and fashioned a couple into spears.

"Whoa! Got one," Denis shouted, and held up an impaled, plump frog on the end of his spear. "Nice fat one."

"Decent!" We exclaimed.

"We need a lot more than that for lunch, ay," Verdie said. So we switched from harvesting cattails to hauling in bullfrogs, tossing them into a great pile on the bank. Soon we had enough for a lunch of frog legs to cook back at the fort later that day.

"I say its race time!" Craig shouted. We grinned at each other, and began the extraordinary game we had invented called 'the bloated frog race'. Carefully and quietly, Craig crouched closer to the green pond scum that blanketed the pond's surface in a flakey, course cover we called frog spit. He gently spread the thick covering apart until he could see into the bronze water. There, below the shallow, stained water rested a spotted bullfrog of gargantuan size. With the precision of a surgeon, he reached down and cradled the frog in his hand, and lifted it to the surface. Holding the mesmerized amphibian in one hand, and with his other hand, carefully inserted a hollow weed into the frog's butt hole.

"Here's a little breath of fresh air, my little friend," he said as he forced a puff of air down the straw into the frog. "Decent. Mines ready," he said, proudly holding his bloated frog. When all of us had our race entries properly inflated we released the amphibious dirigibles into the pond where they floated, and paddled about helplessly without certain direction. There never was a winner in the contest, only glorious laughter and backslapping among the contestants that faded into the midday, mid-June air.

Chapter 5
The Encounter

    Under a tiring sun we plowed through the maze of grass and weeds carrying bundles of cattails and bullfrog legs. We were going to roast the legs back at the cool shade of the fort. When we reached Main Street, Oddie O'Connor, and his brother, Burley, were driving up town with their empty, horse drawn wagon that would be filled with coal at the granary. The clip-clop cadence of Molly's trot was slow enough for us to catch up and hitch a ride in the gray, wooden wagon bed.

    "Hop on fellas," Burley said past a bulging cheek of Red Man chew. The O'Connor brothers lived four miles outside of town on Porter Road, in a dull yellow, wood sided farmhouse. When their day's work was complete, they sat beneath a comfortably pillared porch throughout the late evening on rocking chairs, and drank rye whiskey from tall glasses. The two bachelors had thirty head of Guernsey milkers, and sold their daily gathering to Karsten's Dairy. Their lives were uncomplicated, but laddened with arduous farm chores. A daily dose of rye seemed necessary as they rocked back and forth gazing out across the long shadows of a slumbering evening. Like watching a fire burning, the entrancement of the golden hayfield of their east forty held them in a spell-like stare for hours until the reality of their early morning routine sent them to bed.

    The horse and wagon carried us with a slow, dutiful purpose past Charlie Roseum's Barber Shop. A gray-haired customer clad in a white apron leaned in his pumped up chair to peak at us through a dirty bay window. Across the street, three boys ran from a pair of flung open doors of the Five and Dime store carrying handfuls of small, plastic wrapped candy. Following them was the distraught and furious clerk, Miss Dubois. "Stop! Thief! Stop! You didn't pay for that. I'll call the police!" Miss Dubois screamed, and shook her fist like she was hammering a nail. It was Millender, Manton and Pratt carrying out a candy heist. Down Main Street they ran, giggling and laughing in defiance of the shaken clerk.

    "Piss off, you old hag," Pratt screamed in return. "You can't catch us. Ha, ha!"

    Within a few leaping steps they noticed us riding in the wagon, and cast glares with frowns etched across their sweaty foreheads. We stared back defiantly. A stare returned was a certain invitation to a confrontation. Even a quick glance was enough to challenge someone in Chandlerville, especially the Frenchtown gang. It was too late; the stares were cast, and were made personal now. The three of them stopped abruptly after receiving our dare stares. Then it began. Pratt, hacking up a mouthful of nicotine stained mucous, hurled it toward us through a slimy, waft of spit. He waived a pointed finger like a spray gun covering each of us, and swung his arm and finger below his chin making a mocking motion of a knife slicing his throat. "That's what's waitin' for yous guys," he said with a cold, terrifying look.

"Yeah, we know where to find yous, too," Millender said while shaking a threatening fist at us.

With that gesture, Denis rose from the wagon bed in a motion of valor like a dormant phoenix. He thrust a cattail-clutching fist rebelliously toward the sky, and returned a scowled look of insubordination. Turning his backside to the three villains, he bent forward and with a summonsing grunt he let loose a billowing flatulence of gas that made the O'Connells grin and the villains take a step backward. Pratt and Millender started toward us with their arms held rigidly to their sides. "Come on guys. Let's get the hell outta here!" Manton hollered while grabbing at both of them and casting what seemed like an apologetic glance at us.

Was that a breach in his toughness, I thought? I hoped. Off they ran like rats at the dump, clutching arms full of candy, and carrying on with hoots and hollers. Like dime store bandits they disappeared down an alley headed toward the safety of Frenchtown.

What had we started? Did we start it? Denis didn't care, I know. I felt safe having him on our side, and I knew Verdie would devise a wise plan for the day it would all come down. I guess it was only a matter of time before there was a convergence of the two rival parties. Good versus evil was how we looked at it; we were the good ones. But now, we knew that a rumble was sure to happen. Where, we pondered? Whose ground would this epic battle be fought upon? When was it to happen?

Back in the safety of the fort, Craig reached for the burlap door. "Wait, wait, the bucket!" we screamed. It was too late as he flipped the burlap open to a shower of ripe urine that cascaded over top of his head and the bucket clanged with an empty ring at his feet.

"Oh, Christ!" He shouted as he stood in the doorway drenched in his now yellow tee shirt. This wasn't the first time he had forgotten about the piss bucket. He turned and ran across the field to his house where he undressed in the backyard and rinsed himself with a garden hose then changed his clothes and returned.

We huddled around the wood-burning stove. A small fire crackled and puffed, and we toasted our frog leg delicacies skewered to debarked saplings in the open flames. Faces fixed on flame, and frog, we sat solemnly nibbling on the salted, tender, tasty flesh of our harvest, and quietly pondered the Frenchtown gang dilemma.

Chapter 6
Prayers and Performances

...ss the quiet rooftops and
lawn... ...cs of twinkling porch lights
dott... ...n the distance. Faint voices and
do... ...ening as children and pets were
ca... ...field on M-211, 18-year-old
T... ...ding John Deere tractor slowly in a
s... ...ake through a first cutting of hay.
... ...nbling rake left long, folded rows of
... ...g to lie drying in the summer sun
... ...g.

...pper table. Mom was always trying to
... ...nner. She was raised in the Corktown
distr... ...e Great Depression when food and
money were scar... ...arned how to make meals from the
simplest fare, like chicken gizzard stew, goulash from the poorest of

beef parts, head cheese from even more unpleasant ingredients. Tonight's special concoction was going to be a new entre.

Mom lowered the heavy cast iron door of the wood burning stove, and slid a heaping pan of golden skinned, baked chicken legs onto a thick towel, and set it on the dinner table. A swirled mound of mashed potatoes over flowed from the bowl's rim. Gleaming in a buttery wash, freshly baked bread sat unsliced on a wooden cutting board next to a tub of pale yellow butter. She returned to the stovetop, and retrieved a cast iron pot. Setting it squarely in the center of the table we waited and wondered in great anticipation what gourmand delight would frighten us this evening. We felt the ache of hunger within our empty stomachs but were made to wait. Mom's strict devotion to Catholic rules required us to pause until grace was said. Mom removed her checkered apron and hung it over a cupboard door. Pa stayed in the living room slowly nursing from a bottle of Frankenmuth beer, while watching the Huntley Brinkley Report on television. He never ate meals with us. He said we made him nervous but we knew it was something else that kept him away; a daily habit of warm beer and melancholy daydreams. Mom sat at the end of the table but always invited Pa to join us nevertheless.

We lowered our heads and recited in unison, "Bless us O Lord, and these thy gifts which we are about to receive from thy bounty, through Christ, our Lord, Amen!" Finishing with a hasty sign of the cross we filled our plates with succulent drumsticks covered in crusty corn flakes, fresh butter on bread, and mashed potatoes with a rich pool of volcanic, melting butter streaming over its peak. Then, as proudly as a kid displaying a completed model airplane, Mom lifted the lid of the cast iron pot and dug deep into the caldron with a wooden ladle. Out from the pot rose a claw, and then another that revealed a boney, scaly appendage that was held together with sinew and skin. It was chicken foot soup. She, watchfully, poured the pungent broth and feet into each of our bowls, and with a gleam on her face she said, "Whadaya think, boys? Chicken foot soup! Umm." Without pause, she sat down at the table, and carried on as though nothing was unusual.

"Father Klein called and wants you boys to serve mass with him on Sunday. I washed your cassocks and they are hanging on the back porch. Have you been practicing your Latin?"

"Yes," I replied with my fingers crossed, and trying to take the attention away from the grisly chicken foot bowl that sat in front of me. "Denis can say his responses backwards," I added with a preposterous exaggeration.

Denis looked befuddled for a moment. Then, like a balloon being inflated, he began swallowing large gulps of air deep into his stomach until he could swallow no more. Suddenly, a guttural and cavernous voice emerged from his stomach in a continuous belch of incoherent made up words that were supposed to sound like Latin spoken backwards. "E pluribus unim som de spec day um oh ma godda! Inna minna she doon wanna," he blurted in a low, resonant and frightening roar.

We began laughing uncontrollably as food sprayed from our mouths. Mom, bewildered but impressed, said with a puzzled rejoinder, "Very good, Denis?"

"See? I told you we been studying," I said confidently.

"I'm so proud of you boys. I've invited the Dorsey's over for rosary novena tonight." Mom had been going to church every morning, and she was on her ninth and final day of her vigil of prayer in honor of the Blessed Virgin Mary. "They'll be here at seven-thirty, such a wonderful family, and those girls are so adorable. You boys should take notice," she remarked with a wink, but we were ahead of her on that advice.

The three Dorsey girls arrived with their mother, Charlotte, a slender woman in a pale blue dress, and a ruffled, white lace blouse that hung across her frail palms. She was of strong faith, and a member of the Altar Society with my mother. We waited excitedly as we heard their footsteps coming closer up the long stairway that ended in a dark hallway at our apartment door. The young girls were our ages; Sharon was Verdie's age, Susan was Denis' and Donna was my age. Donna's long, blond curls hung perfectly about her pale face like delicate coils of Spanish moss. She spoke quietly and bashfully with her chin held downward when we recited the rosary. We kneeled throughout the nine rosaries on thin carpet with our backs straight as fence posts. There would be no slouching position because it was slightly sacrilegious in my mother's eyes. Kneeling for so long was painful, and boring, but we put forward our best pious posture in prayer to impress the Dorseys. Mom's novena was now complete.

The girls were prim, proper and pretty, and in their presence my brothers and I were instantly overcome with ostentatious claims of bravado and achievement. "I climbed to the top of the willow down by the Ruins today," I boasted. "Had to fetch Flossie Fairchild's cat. I got a couple of scratches on my arm. See?" I said as I pulled up my sleeve to show Donna some marks left on my arm from wrestling with Denis earlier that day. "That cat was so happy to have me pluck it from certain doom it dug right into my arm to get a good hold on me." I smiled while invoking the two fingers crossed behind my back that I was getting good at. Denis held back a giggle.

"Verdie, how about drawing a picture for us?" Mom asked bluntly. She was invariably putting us on the spot to perform in some display that would reveal our talent. She picked up a long sketchpad and handed it to Verdie.

"Aw, all right." Verdie said sheepishly but with a willingness that wasn't in true protest.

Now, it was Verdie's turn to show his skill. He sat on the couch quietly with the sketchpad, and a clutch of number 1, 2 and 3 pencils on his lap. Sharon was sitting across the room on a high back, velour chair with her slender legs crossed, and her arms piously folded across her lap. Verdie, furtively, glanced her way while drawing her portrait. Susan sat disinterested on a stool, and fussed with her rosary.

"While Verdie draws up something for us I think we should hear from Denis," Mom said, looking down at him where he sat shrinking in his chair. "Come on Denis; sing that preacher and the bear song. You know that Phil Harris song you like to sing? I hear you sing it all the time." Verdie and I chimed in excitedly because we knew he had a good voice, and knew all of the lyrics. He had practiced and constructed a dance routine in front of the bathroom mirror, and we would see a complete chorographical display along with his song. Denis lifted himself from his chair, and with his chin held upward like actors do on stage, stepped to the center of the room where he paused for a moment, then began his performance.

"The preacher went out walking, was on a Sunday morn.
T'was against his religion but he brought his gun along.
He shot himself some mighty fine quail and one little measly hare
But on his way returning home he met a great big Grisly bear."

On and on went the lyrics sung in key by an animated, bodacious Denis. In a Vaudevillian like display he casted his arms outward in flailing motions accentuating the different nuances of the song. Our guests sat bright-eyed, entranced by his performance. Nearing the end of his act a subtle look of discomfort came across his face as he squinted slightly through a taught, furrowed frown. This was not part of his skit. He reached the end of his animated recital, and the room erupted in grand applause. Charlotte Dorsey rose from her chair, and clapped in enthusiastic approval, "Bravo, Bravo!" Denis stood very still, and looked very pale, but summoned a queasy smile.

"Take a bow, Denis." Mom urged, "That's what all performers do after such a great display of talent. Come on now, take your bow."

"Well, I. I don't think I should. You know it wouldn't be right and all." Denis said in an uncomfortable stammer. What we didn't know was that in his earlier performance of backwards Latin all of the ingested air had not been released. There, inside his prodigious plumbing, a gaseous gathering awaited escape.

"Take your bow, Denis!" Mom said more directly, like an order.

"Ah, all right then," Denis, said sheepishly, and without further delay he crossed his right arm below his waist and bent forward in a bow. There, in a raucous display of flatulence, the pent up air escaped in a humiliating tumult. Hands were clamped across astonished faces in hasty defense, eyes were shuttered in amazement as the humiliated, and apologetic Denis retreated from the living room. In his hurried departure blurbs of bleating blats continued with each hasty step he took toward the shelter of the bathroom. Verdie and I looked at each other thinking 'what did ya expect'.

Like a curtain drawing across a frantic stage, Verdie quickly changed the flabbergasted mood of the audience with an unveiling of his work of art. He held up the sketchpad for all to view. "This is for you," he said, bolstered with pride in his presentation to Sharon. There was Sharon, revealed in amazing facial accuracy with the soft blending of the varied pencils highlighting her hair, and a hint of a gentle smile on her face. Upon closer review, and probably brought forth through some subliminal reference to the chicken foot soup, were two beastly claws approaching her neck like a creature from a horror movie. Sharon blushed in appreciation, not noticing the menacing accoutrement to her portrait.

"Oh, thank you so much, Verdun." A smitten Sharon said while rolling the portrait into a tight, spiral coil.

The eventful evening came to a close when the phone rang. It was a 'call'.

Chapter 7
The Call

    The Dorseys had gracefully departed our humble home now, but left with the indelible experience of an unforgettable evening. It was 9 o'clock in the pale evening, and my brothers and I retreated to our bedroom awaiting the outcome of the call. We were not allowed to use the phone. It was a business phone for receiving calls from hospitals, nursing homes, police departments, coroners, and grieving families. Whenever it rang we abruptly stopped in whatever we were doing because the high-pitched bell might mean someone had died.

    Mom held the clumsy, yellow handle of the phone closely between her ear and shoulder and took notes from Lloyd Levin, the Chief of Police. Pa, downstairs in the funeral parlor listened on another extension. She placed the phone back in its cradle, and leaned against the doorway to the living room. She breathed a heartrending sigh, and placed a hand on her mournful forehead. She wiped at a gathering of tears that had collected around her eyes, "Hail Mary full of Grace," she recited in a shallow whisper then completed her notes in an attempt at equanimity. We never used the word 'died' to state the death of someone; we referred to it as a 'call'. Someone had taken a final breath that evening in Chandlerville.

We had become familiar with the sounds and patterns of each other's footsteps when we climbed the tall stairwell, recognizable as our voices when one of us made our way up and down the long, exhausting climb. From our bedroom we heard the familiar sound of Pa's feet thumping atop the creaking rises in slow, shuffling steps making his way to the apartment.

"I'll need da boys on dis one," Pa said to Mom directly when he entered the living room. "He's a big, heavyset boy, and he'll be hard to carry. I'll need 'dem to help lift him on da table, too," Pa slowly shook his head in a dispirited tone.

"It breaks my heart to press the boys into this," Mom sighed.

"Such an awful accident. I hope Harley and Delores Maddox aren't out there when we pick him up. They shouldn't have to see this," Pa said. The Maddox's were members of our church, and we bought fresh eggs from them occasionally. Mom held her clenched hands around a damp handkerchief, and looked our way in a tearful glance when we headed for the hearse.

We walked down the alley and slid onto the wide bench seat sitting four abreast. The blue Ford hearse was used as a body pick-up vehicle, a hearse for funerals and an ambulance. Pa drove away and made a wide, sweeping turn at the corner of Main Street, and onto M-211. Gray Hartman was standing at the corner past the gas pumps of his Standard Gas Station. He held a greasy rag in his hand, and looked down M-211 toward the Maddox farm that was only a mile up the road. He gave us an abrupt look and slowly shook his head as we went past him. Word of the accident had spread quickly as it always did when there was a call.

A few cars were parked along the highway as we approached the hayfield. A red light slowly spun atop Lloyd Levin's Plymouth Fury police car. Doc Finch, the local doctor and coroner of the county, hadn't arrived yet. He was delivering Kate Henderson's baby boy at the town's small hospital. Chic Vermont's Chevy pickup was parked alongside the tractor and hay rake. His washed out straw hat was tilted back on his head. A faded glow of the late evening sun spilled across the hat's tan line on his solemn forehead. Buck Russell, a neighboring farmer was standing next to him with his giant arms folded across his blue jean bibs, with a pale, remorseful look on his face. Vermont spoke, "Iyes comin down 211 an seen the John Deere out there in the field jus goin kinna drivin' in a circle catty wampus ta the hay rows. I knew sompin was wrong, there wunt no one drivin' er," he paused, and scratched his ear, then readjusted his hat, "Don't know why he would leave that pto runnin'. Problee got his shirt caught in the spinnin' rake. Pulled him right in. Damn! He'd run that rig many a time. Just shouldna happened."

Buck Russell put his right foot atop the tractor's front wheel, and leaned forward. He pointed with a weathered, heavily knuckled finger across M-211, "Iyes cutting across the road on my south forty. Was getting late, and sumpin weren't right I thought, too. The boy'd been mowin' an rakin' all afternoon, an' I seen Harley drive out 'round six ta bring em some supper. Didn't pay much mind til Iyes done, an' that Deer was still thumpin' out there in the field. Chic, an' I got here 'bout the same time. Poor kid, musta tried clearin' the gearbox.. Spines grabbed 'em, an jus speard tha hell outta 'em. Chain finally jumped a gear, and stopped spinnin'. Found em stuck to the rakes, an' the tractor still chuggin' along. Had a hellova time catchin' the tractor, an pryin 'em lose, Wunt breathin, and blud all 'round," Russell said, and looked back at a yellow Ford flatbed pickup truck that was parked in the field with its headlights beaming onto the nearby maple tree line. Two figures sat holding each other in empty stares while looking out across the hay stubble; it was Harley and Delores Maddox.

Doc Finch had arrived, and took his stethoscope from a black medical bag. Timothy Maddox lay sprawled on the hay stubble near the tractor. His arms and legs were spread apart as though he was about to make a snow angel. My brothers and I stood like small soldiers in the shadows waiting for the official word from Doc Finch. The Doc removed Vermont's blue Mackinaw jacket that was spread across Timothy's upper body, and face. He unbuttoned the green, plaid shirt to reveal Timothy's chest. The tines made small red dotted puncture holes about his chest, arms and head. There was no sound coming from Timothy's chest as he moved the scope's rubber cup several places on his bloodied torso. Drips of blood continued to ooze from the injuries when he finished his examination. With a shake of his head, he motioned to us with a circular wave.

We parked the gurney beside Timothy. Pa took his right arm, Verdie and Denis each took a leg, and I bent down and tried for a firm grip on his left wrist. His body was unpleasantly warm even after an hour of lying in the field. His bulky body sagged like a sack of grain when we hoisted it onto the cart, and more blood trickled from his wounds. This wasn't the first time we had to get a body at an accident scene, but the apprehension and circumspect that was expected of us through humble piety was intricate.

By now a collection of cars and trucks had gathered near the driveway to the field. Their headlights spraying bright blasts of light onto the layers of blue mist gathering in the night fields. The heavy hearse's undercarriage scraped the gravel as we drove up the steep incline onto M-211. Curious people stood motionless on warm blacktop, and we drove past them feeling important and official on our way to the funeral home.

"A hum," Pa grunted as he tried to conceal the swish of a beer cap being clipped off its bottle. Out in the gloomy hayfield a yellow flatbed drove slowly through the mowed, sweet-smelling hay toward the two-story farmhouse at the end of the field. The next day the Maddox's would come to the funeral home to make final arrangements for Timothy.

Chapter 8
The Shack on the Black

The mid-June days were hot and it hadn't rained for some time. Gardens and lawns took on brown tinges of colorless pedals and blades as sprinklers sprayed waves of water to keep them alive. Inside our fort even the damp clay floor began to crack and wither. Denis sat poised on an empty bucket poking a cattail arrow at an ant that was scurrying in circles avoiding his prodding. Verdie was reading a Mad Magazine while Froggy, Johnny, Craig and I offered suggestions of things to do to breakup our boredom.

"Tuff's Pond?" Someone suggested.

"Nah. Dump and shoot rats?" Another suggested.

"Humm, maybe."

"Ay," a muffled voice came from outside the burlap door. "Yin' there?" It said.

"Yeah. Whosit?" We replied.

"Me, Willie," said the voice, and the burlap door pealed back. Willie Hanson stooped and entered.

Willie was a good friend of Verdie's from school and an honorary member to the fort though infrequent in his attendance until now. He was a year older but they shared the same chemistry class. He lived with his grandparents, Curly and Beulah Hanson. Old Curly was a brilliant gunsmith, and was sought after for his keen ability to make hand checkered gunstocks, and custom scribing on rifle receivers. Verdie, and Willie had very similar interests. On the alley side of the funeral home was a trap door opening that led to a coal bin and basement. We used the trap door as a secret entrance to sneak in and out of the funeral home so our parents wouldn't know when we came or went. The only thing that gave us away was the coal dust on our clothes. On a work counter in the basement, Verdie and Willie built crystal radios and concocted explosive contraptions like pipe bombs, rotten egg gas vessels and miniature rockets made from Ohio Blue Tip matches wrapped in aluminum foil.

Willie entered and stood with his coiled, black hair brushing the planked ceiling. He rubbed his narrow nose with a boney forearm, and inspected the confines with squinting, intelligent eyes that were spread far apart on his pocked forehead. He was slender, and almost scrawny beneath his blue jeans and green tee shirt that hung loosely on his body. "Decent," he declared nodding his head in approval to the amenities we had added since his last visit. He flipped over a bucket and sat amongst us. He folded his spindly arms across his thin chest and began speaking of a delicious discovery he had made while riding through the Pigeon River forest with his grandfather. "Gramps needed some more walnut for stocks, and knew where an old deadfall was laying back by the cee cee railroad grade. We were drivin' over the Clark's Bridge and I see this old shack way down the Black River, kinda hidden in the swale, you could barely see it. So I asked Gramps, what's that old shack? He says, 'That's the old cee cee camp shed where they kept supplies when the government built the railroad through here in the forties.' So I says, what kinda supplies did they keep in that shack? Gramps says, 'Dynamite'".

We leaned forward in intense anticipation and said nothing while our minds whirled at the thought of dynamite and the things we could do with it.

"You yankin' us, Willie?" Verdie said in cautious doubt.

"No, jus' sayin' what Gramps told me," Willie replied.

The fort was surprisingly quiet, and we sat pensively gazing with vacant faces. We were all energized by the thought of an expedition.

"Yanna' take a trip, guys?" Verdie asked with raised eyebrows and high anticipation.

"Shit man, yeah," I said and rubbed my hands together in a sandy swirl.

"O.K., here's what we should do. Get our poles and some crawlers, raid Mom's pantry," Verdie said hurriedly and hastily while coming up with stuff we would need for the journey out to Pigeon River forest, "oh, and matches, we need matches. Chris, you get the sleeping bags, they're in hallway closet."

"No, sleeping bags are too much to carry," I reasoned; "We'll have to just take some of those wool blankets Mom keeps on the back porch, an roll 'em tight."

"Grab some forks, spoons and a couple a knives," Verdie continued.

Oh, the plans that can be made by young boys with wild imaginations of fish on a line, moonlight and campfire light, and the excitement of new properties to explore, and possibly getting our hands on some dynamite. We made mental notes when we received our hasty assignments from Verdie and Willie. A great list of items was compiled in reverence to the Boy Scout mantra 'always be prepared'. So a gathering of fishing poles, knives, spoons, canteens, matches and blankets were about to be collected. A clandestine raid on the families' larder for cans of beans, sardines, soups and crackers was soon undertaken.

Under a late morning, hazy June sun, we scampered from the fort to gather the goods and meet at Willie Hanson's house for our trip to the Pigeon River forest. Craig's parents wouldn't let him go along. They said, it wasn't safe to go out into elk country. Froggy couldn't go, either, his father was putting up firewood for the winter and he was going to stack for him.

So one by one, we trudged through the backstreets of town conspicuously carrying our backpacks, maple sapling bows and clutches of cattail arrows neatly strapped on our backs with binder twine.

We were to meet at Willie's house at the edge of town, on M-68 Highway. Once there we would take the highway west into Cheboygan County, and follow the sandy back roads through the Jack Pine plains to Pigeon River forest.

Like recruits gathering for a military bivouac, some had brown sleeping bags piled high on their shoulders, canvas bindles containing clanking cans of food and metal ware, and fishing poles disassembled and taped together for ease of carry. Verdie, Denis and I were the last ones to show up. We had a bit of convincing to do to get permission from Mom. We repositioned our heavy backpacks on our shoulders and kneeled on a crusty brown lawn for a breather.

Old Curly Bowman stepped from the dimly lit gun shed and squinted through his thick, dirty lenses at our gathering. His white sprawling hair spilled over his temples and seemed to grow from his ears. His waxy sunken cheeks bore white stubble from a couple of weeks of a razors absence. In a low, almost indistinguishable voice he mumbled toward our strange congregation, "You boys up to?" He brushed woodchips from his checkered flannel shirt with a blue veined hand. Brown clusters of age spots were stippled across the tops of hands and forearms where they protruded from his rolled up shirtsleeves. A hand rolled cigarette smoldered between two dark yellow, tobacco-stained fingers, "Campin'?" He asked while a long ash hung from the wrinkled cigarette.

"Wer gonna' fish the Horse Race Rapids on the Black this afternoon, Gramps," Willie replied in a slight embroidery of the truth. We watched anxiously for the ash to drop.

"A few nice hard maples down there in the Spreads. Damn nice stock material, ya' know. Carves real good," he reflected. The long ash, still, hadn't dropped.

"Probly' camp there tonight and head upstream and fish the holes up there," Willie continued.

"When ya' be back, Willard?" Curly said addressing Willie by his full name.

"Couple days," Willie replied as he flung his backpack over his shoulder. We continued to watch in amazement as the defiant ash grew longer and longer, but it was time to leave.

We walked to the highway and looked back at Curly Bowman where he stood in front of his gray gun shack, straining to see us and still holding the beautifully constructed ash on the end of his cigarette.

We hiked along the gravel shoulder of M-68 and held up our thumbs to passing cars. One mile, then two miles without any takers as the sun beat down on us mercilessly. Finally, Macey Maserone rumbled up to us in his white fifty-six Chevy pickup with the radio blaring a Johnny Horton tune, The Battle of New Orleans. We stopped and let out a sigh, and wiped the dripping sweat from our faces, "Finally! Thought no one would ever stop for us," Verdie said while leaning on the driver's door. Maserone sat sprawled across the driver's seat and reached over to the radio and flicked the volume control backward. He worked for the D&M Railroad as a gandy dancer laying track, and it was his day off. He pushed his long slender fingers through his dark hair that was hanging about his handsome face and gave a puzzled gaze at our hapless group, "where ya headed?"

"Clark's Bridge," we said.

"Can take ya' as far as Buzzel's farm," he offered generously.

"Decent," we responded.

"Thirsty?" he asked while tapping his knee to the tune crackling through the dashboard speaker.

"Thirsty as hell! Thirsty as hell! Yeah, yeah!" We suddenly discovered.

He thought for a moment, "shit damn," Macey cried, as he slapped at the black steering wheel; "might jus' as well drop yas' at the crock in the road!" His charitable offer was met with a chorus of profound exclamations of, "decent, decent, decent!" Not only would his lift bring us within a couple of miles of the Clark's Bridge but a delightful quenching of our parched bodies at the 'crock in the road' spring.

We hastily peeled the cumbersome cargo from our backs and flung them into the pickup. Hoisting ourselves over the sides of the dented pickup box, we took up seats along its cool, metal walls. Willie sat leaning against his bindle with his knees pulled tight to his chest and his arms dangling long and thin. Johnny Harkins was sitting across from Verdie, Denis and me with his legs over top of each other. On each foot was mismatched, untied, PF Flyer tennis shoe bearing marks of raucous wear on their smooth soles. We were misfits on a mission of discovery.

Down the gravel road Maserone's pickup sped. Blossoming clouds of gray dust filled the back of the truck and settled in our hair and on our laps. We said nothing as we listened to the radio faintly playing a Bobby Darin tune. Our heads bobbled back and forth like dashboard dolls with every undulation of the dry road.

The crock in the road was coming up and Macey slid the wobbly shifter on the steering column into second gear. The six-banger engine rumbled in a high pitch rev, and the truck slid to a dusty stop. We rose from the wood plank bed and slapped the gritty powder from our clothes.

"Yo' kay right here?" Macey asked with a splintered toothpick hanging from the side of his mouth.

"Man, can't thank ya' enough," Willie said; "Saved us a ton a time, Macey."

"No prob'. Don't let the elk and the bear feed on yous," he said while coughing out a laugh.

"They broke the mold when they made you, buddy," Willie said with a sweaty grin.

"Yeah, and there's a place in heaven waitin' for me, too," he said while pointing his mashed toothpick our way. He slammed the shifter into first gear with a screeching grind. The engine screamed in a high-pitched roar and he dumped the clutch while cutting the wheel hard to the right. The truck swung violently in a semi-circle with its back tires flinging sand and gravel, leaving prodigious trenches in the road. Off he went in his white Chevy truck peeling back and forth in a controlled fishtail until he became a white dot heading out of sight.

The babbling of cold, gushing water from the crock invited us to drink. Shaded by a stringy willow that hung overhead, we took turns burying our faces into the chilled wave of water that gurgled up from a galvanized pipe as it had done since the work crews of the Civilian Conservation Corp hand drove the well in the 1940s. We filled our canvas-clad canteens and twisted their aluminum caps tightly closed. Our hands stung from the chilly water despite the heat of the midday sun. Scraggly, shadeless Jack Pines towered above us breathlessly null of any breeze.

The gravel road changed into a two-tracker of dry yellow sand and our feet sunk into the fine golden grains with every spongy step. The hiking was difficult, but we plowed along toward the bridge. A constant swarm of mosquitoes, gnats, black flies and purple dragonflies buzzed about our clammy foreheads and we swatted at them subconsciously. Johnny hummed the last song that played on Macey's radio, "Splish Splash". The terrain gradually changed from pine forest into green canopies of sugar maples, slender poplars and white cedar with fleshy bark peeling away from their trunks. We were close to the river now.

We reached the bridge, and paused in long sighs, then dropped our gear on the deck. Below us the Black River rushed past in an ancient dark flow. Deadfall cedars lay partially submerged with their clusters of roots defiantly clinging to the banks, and the swift current spilling over them made swirling whirlpools of gray - white foam. We looked upstream to the place where Willie saw the shack. There it was sitting conspicuously planted amidst the yellow swale grass in a brief opening in the cedar swamp. A rusty metal roof still protected the shack and glowed in the sunlight. We leaned against the steel braces of the bridge on our hands and knees and studied it in silence. The suspense finally overtook us, and we made our way to the shack through the thick swale and blow downs along the riverbank.

Willie was the first one to step onto the shack's short porch. Broken deck boards curled up at our feet, and some were rotted through. The shack stood with a slight lean, and the door was difficult to open when he held the metal lever down and pushed. The door bound itself on the uneven floor but with Verdie's help they managed to swing it open. In the darkness a ground squirrel scampered off through a hole in the wall, and the floor was messy with old newspapers, tin cans and animal droppings. "Man!" Willie said as he strained to take in the entirety of the room; "What a hell hole," he said as all of us stepped into the musty shack.

"Look at this," I said as I edged closer to a grey partition where writing was scrawled haphazardly on the pine board walls. Verdie pulled a candle from his bindle and lit the waxy wick with a stiff Ohio Blue Tip. There, revealed in the flickering candlelight, were signatures sprawled in jagged script and illegible letters of those who once gathered there. There were names like Bucky Dawson, Boss Karsten, Wes Chapman and Ferris Hancock. High on the wall read an inscription left by some lamenting ghost of the past:

"Here, there, and everywhere lies Rudy Langworthy. Shoulda been careful with his cigarette"

In hesitant thought, after reading the inscription, we glanced about the room furtively as though we might see fragments of Rudy Langworthy plastered on the walls. Finally, we laughed timidly at the ill-omened message.

"Well, so much for finding dynamite," Denis shrugged and walked from the shack into the bright afternoon sun. He sat on the step of the rickety deck and began to assemble his fishing pole. Johnny sat beside him, so did Verdie and Willie. I remained in the shack with the candle flickering faintly for further exploration. I kicked at the brown newspapers that lay on the floor. Some were dated 1950, 1951 and earlier. One headline read, "Marines Retreat From 38th Parallel." In a dusty corner a feeble wooden table stood against cobweb cluttered walls, and an opened Campbell Beans can lay on its rusty side. Below the table a perfectly square wooden frame broke the continuity of the flooring. I stepped to the table and slide it to the side to reveal the boxed frame that lay beneath it. There, reset into the frame, a hole had been drilled and bore the smooth marks of dirty fingers that had reached into it many times to remove it. It was a trap door framed into the greater floor.

"What the hang is this, guys?" I said with uncertain optimism. I heard a flood of footsteps coming from behind, and the other boys were now standing at my side where I knelt. I placed my dirty finger into the dusty hole and gave a forceful pull. The frame began to separate and break free from its resting place and popped above the floor. I slid the frame to one side and looked into the dark cavern. Lying below me rested a dusty wooden box covered with cobwebs and fine debris that had sifted on top of it. On my stomach, I brushed away the dust and faint letters appeared in dull black, ornate type across the wooden lid. It read: Gold Medal Dynamite-High Explosives-Dangerous. These were the words we craved to read! Better than reading a Mark Twain novel, and more exciting than watching Mister Ed on TV: Dynamite! High explosives! Dangerous! A chill went through my body in the hot stagnant room as I read out loud. The salty drippings from my forehead burned my eyes as we gazed at the wondrous treasure. The others plunked themselves down on the debris on the floor and smiled in unrestrained glee. Resting next to the twenty-five pound box was a tight coil of Primacord Blasting Fuse. We sat curled up on the wood planking and peered down into the dark opening with the wax candle drippings flowing down its stem, then someone said in a hushed release, "Decent."

Chapter 9
The Business of Kittens

    Flossie Fairchild sat on a crimson cloth-covered stool finalizing the white curls in her hair before the oval shaped mirror in her bedroom. Tilting her head from side to side and turning her face in different angles she studied the results of her recent trip to Claire's Beauty Salon. Looking past her wrinkled cheeks and sagging chin folds, she dabbed an ivory handled brush purposely about her head. "That looks good," she whispered to herself. Flossie was an eighty-year-old retired English teacher from Chandlerville High School. Her husband, Rand, had died a decade earlier and she lived with her calico cat, Miss Puss, in a bright white two-story behind Harrington's Pool Hall. In chance encounters with us she still corrected our English with helpful reminders of, "Has seen, not saw;" or "Ain't is not a word, for heaven's sake." Sometimes, we would purposely construct cockeyed, triple negative sentences like, "we don't got none no more," just to watch her heavily jowled face wince and contort in frustration. On a romantic moon filled night, months earlier, Miss Puss had escaped Flossie's protective chastity to partake in a midnight soirée with an ignoble alley tom. The results of the ephemeral romance produced a litter of six multicolored kittens. This prompted her to call her nephew, Butch Hopkins, owner of Hopkins's Granary who promised to send someone by to gather and place the unwanted kittens in 'good homes'. The piercing whistle of a tea pot sang loudly in her kitchen and Flossie poured its boiling water over a couple of A&P tea bags. Miss Puss lay curled up in a cardboard box in the pantry fussing about her kittens. She carried the dainty cup and saucer to her sitting room and placed herself on a tall backed green chair and took hesitant sips from the cup. Miss Puss came from the pantry and leaped upon Flossie's lap and purred comfortably.

"There now, everything is going to be just fine as wine," she said while stroking her hand down the cat's yellow back. She heard the footsteps of a visitor crossing her wainscot covered porch and saw a dark figure peering through the glass of her front door. A hard knuckle thumped loudly and rattled the glass in the door. Flossie walked excitedly toward the entrance believing that her nephew had sent the visitor to rescue her from the unwanted felines. She hastily opened the door. There stood a mucky faced teen wearing his blue jeans rolled up at the cuffs, a soiled white tee shirt with a pack of Camel's twisted tightly into a sleeve and brightly polished black pointed shoes. His dull black hair was shaped into a V that tumbled onto his forehead. It was Bill Pratt. Standing at the foot of Flossie's concrete sidewalk stood Fred Millender and Buckshot O'Toole waiting impatiently for Pratt.

"Are you..." Flossie began to ask.

"Pratt. Bill Pratt, and I heard you had some cats ta get rid a," Pratt said. He had overheard Butch Hopkins talking to Flossie about her kitten dilemma while he was in the granary trying to steal a Milky Way from a counter display. Hopkins wouldn't have sent Pratt because he knew what sort of character he was, especially when he caught him stealing the candy bar. Hopkins raced sled dogs and had a slew of Siberian Huskies he kenneled behind the granary. The dogs barked constantly and Pratt hated them. One day the barking ceased and Hopkins found all of his dogs dead in their kennel. They had been poisoned and Hopkins believed it was Pratt who was responsible.

"Why, yes I do. Now, I want to make sure that you are going to place these precious kittens in fine homes. That is what you do, isn't it?" Flossie said.

"Fifty cents apiece," Pratt said while crossing his hairy arms over his defiant chest. "You can count on it, Mam. Dunnit a bunch a times," of course Pratt had no intention of placing the kittens in 'good homes'. While other industrious kids from town had jobs like mowing lawns, paper routes delivering The Detroit Free Press or hawking Grit Magazine in the local bars, Pratt formulated his own form of commerce. Instead of a respectable job, he conducted a dubious and grisly business of duping customers into believing he was a savior who would diligently find homes for their kittens and puppies. When, instead, he was in the business of cruelty by brutally torturing and destroying the animals while charging a fee. Flossie Fairchild, naïvely fetched her purse and the box of doomed kittens. Pratt stuffed the box under his arm and the dollars in his pocket and bowed to Flossie as he retreated from the vestibule and returned to his impatient friends on the sidewalk. They marched down Spruce Street like a murderous, truant posse heading for the stone quarry where they would conduct their gruesome affair.

The Chandlerville Limestone Company was on the north outskirts of town, next to the D&M railroad tracks and behind the Hopkins Granary. There were enormous veins of iron-stained limestone unearthed by men clinging to noisy jackhammers and pick axes. Froggy's father, Newton, worked there mining large sheets of stone. The deep voids where stone was removed made perfect ponds filled with green ground water and were enticing to us on hot summer days. All we had to do was sneak past the 'Danger-No Trespassing' signs, just like Mary Manton had done the day she drowned.

Pratt and his crew sneaked across the tracks like a pack of trespassing coyotes and into the seclusion of the quarry carrying the box of kittens. A path had been made by countless footsteps going back and forth from the ponds. There was an opening just over the bank of the railroad grade that had large boulders and sheets of limestone shards in menacing shapes protruding from of the ground. Familiar surnames and ambiguous messages of vulgarity had been spray-painted on some of the rocks in an assortment of colors. This was the lair of the Frenchtown Gang. There was a shallow pit in the center of the opening that held ashes and pieces of charred wood from countless fires made by the gang. Pratt, Millender and O'Toole gathered by the pit and placed the box on the ground. "I sure had her bullshitted," Pratt boasted to the others as he knelt on one knee and pulled a kitten from the box. Cradling the kitten in one hand and holding it up to thoroughly inspect it like he was making a purchase he walked to a nearby boulder. Standing like a pitcher on a mound he leaned forward with his left arm reaching down to his left knee. He bent his right arm behind his back with the kitten held firmly in his closed fist and glared at the limestone boulder ten feet in front of him.

"The count is three balls and two strikes. Pratt leans in to get the sign from his catcher, he shakes his head then he nods... fastball it is," In a windup and a furious release the kitten was thrown end over end against the boulder where it died instantly. O'Toole, picked up a blunt piece of firewood and cheered, "hellova throw, but watch this," and he took a batter's stance in front of the boulder and waited for the next kitten to be thrown. Without remorse, he and Millender took turns smashing the helpless kittens until they were all bludgeoned to death. A fire was made in the pit and the box of mangled kittens was placed into the flames. Neither Flossie nor Miss Puss would ever know the fate of those 'precious' kittens as Pratt and his gang departed the lair to swim in the green ponds of the quarry.

Chapter 10
The Uncomfortable Encounter

    Benny McCain squatted and retrieved a brown bottle from the nap of overgrown weeds in the ditch along Hutchinson Highway. The bottle clinked against the others he had collected when he stuffed it into his knapsack. In a bent over walk, from a once broken back, he continued his expedition along the dusty roadways outside of town. Clad in brown baggy trousers held up by frayed striped suspenders that stretched over a faded blue cotton short-sleeve shirt, he moseyed carefully through the ditches of the county collecting two-cent returns and anything else he knew he could sell to Bill Fassbinder. A faded blue Detroit Tigers baseball cap fit loosely on his balding head and displayed wavy lines of countless soakings of sweat. McCain lived alone in a tin sided shack on County Line Road on the outskirts of Chandlerville. He kept to himself and had no friends that checked in on him where he lived like a hermit. Townsfolk would see him walk by in his shadowy trek toward Fassbinder's and remark, "He must have a ton a money out there in that shack." Benny McCain was rarely seen in the town stores, only an occasional trip to Leed's Grocery Store and then, like a phantom, he was gone again. McCain had been a constant character around town for years where he came and went from Fassbinder's cashing in his humble trove of discards he gathered throughout the county. Like a mysterious blur of dust he quietly breezed through the alleys and side streets; a lonesome wayward traveler never speaking to anyone. But he knew many of the town's dark secrets that he witnessed during his wanderings. Occasionally, people had observed the mysterious McCain burying items in his front yard prompting them to believe that this is where he kept his fortune. Next to his shack was an earth cellar with a trap door poorly obscured by clusters of branches and brush that he sneaked out to at all times of the day and night. He waited politely at the double doors of Leed's Grocery as Rhiney Buza walked through and stopped briefly.

"McCain, what the hell brings you ta the store, out a toilet paper 'er somp 'un?"

McCain lowered his chin in no reply. His eyes darted uncomfortably about the door's entrance. Rhiney Buza owned a saw mill in the village of Afton that was ten miles west of Chandlerville, in Cheboygan County. He had the personality of a pig rooting in barnyard mud and wasn't bashful about asking the most indelicate question. He developed his powerful lean build from hoisting heavy logs all day making him an imposing figure at the entrance, blocking McCain's path.

"Good day, sir," McCain humbly replied.

"Say, I hear ya' got loads a dough out there at yer shack?" Buza said with a push of his meaty hand to McCain's shoulder.

"Where the hell ya' keep it anyway? Better be careful, Mister. Never know about these kids 'round here if they ever get wind of it." McCain politely brushed past him and hastily walked into the store avoiding further intrusion.

In the store a demure Dave Manton pushed a squeaky wheel cart through a narrow isle of canned vegetables and paused to remove two cans of beans. His mother sent him to the store and his cart was devoid of frivolous purchase. Only staples could be bought with the few food stamps his mother possessed. From behind he heard a familiar voice. "Hello, David. I am so happy to see you. I have been very worried about you and miss you immensely," the diminutive voice said. Manton stiffened and grasped the handle of the cart tightly and didn't turn to face the person who was now standing directly beside him.

"I'm fine," Manton bristled in a cautious and defiant reply to the figure that was dressed in a black cassock and starched white collar. It was Father Klein.

"I have been praying for your return to the church, David. I miss our chats and drives out into the country. You know I have a new car now. It's very stylish and very responsive and drives like a dream. I would love for you to drive it," the priest offered through a soft and almost sultry voice of indistinct temptation to the disinterested Manton.

In a forced glance, Manton turned to Father Klein and narrowed his eyelids in reply, "Leave me alone! I don't want anything to do with you or your fuckin' new car."

"Please don't be that way, David," the apologetic priest said while reaching into his pocket to retrieve a handful of crumpled money. "Here, please take this to help with your purchase."

Manton, not taking the money, sped away in a hasty jerk of the squeaky cart, and briskly wheeled down the isle of cans to the checkout clerk. He turned his head halfway back toward the dejected priest; "Don't ever talk to me again!"

In one isle over from this unsettling encounter, Benny McCain quietly observed and studied the rows of goods that were neatly placed on the shelves. Father Klein remained for a moment in embarrassment, hoping no one had overheard the unpleasant exchange with Manton. Stoically, he retreated in a pious posture and strolled to the meat counter where a frugal Blanche Merritt, the church organist and frequently out of key vocalist, was squeezing packages of chicken. "What a marvelous rendition last Sunday, Blanche," the priest said as he approached her with a slightly reddened face.

"Oh, thank you, Father. I try," the blushing organist replied; "And what did you think of my singing Ave Maria?" Merritt begged. "You will remember me for the lead vocals for our Christmas presentation, won't you?"

"That was wonderful, too, and yes, I will think of you for the lead, Blanche," the priest replied while deliberately concealing his crossed fingers behind his black cassock.

Dave Manton, cans in hand, flew through the double doors and trotted down Main Street heading toward Frenchtown. McCain, clutching his brown paper sack silently slipped out the back entrance of the store where he disappeared like a fading rain cloud. Blanche Merritt pushed her loaded cart quickly behind a retreating black cassock in a further attempt to garner the lead vocals for the Christmas presentation that was months away. The priest hastily opened the door of his shiny red Thunderbird and twisted the ignition key, nodding and smiling politely in his attempt to flee from the persistent choir singer.

Chapter 11
The Red Shirt

'Chandlerville Steers The World', a bright blue and red placard proclaimed in bold letters where it hung on a cinderblock wall of the Chandlerville News. The pinging bell of an Underwood Typewriter carriage traveling quickly back and forth across a sheet of paper rang out at the end of each line. Harold 'Scoop' Burnham fervently stabbed at its shiny black and white keys. Beside him, 'Flight of the Bumblebee' raced in a scratchy cadence on a tired phonograph as he pecked and plunked at the keys in unison to the fervid melody. Stopping for a moment, with eyes closed, he waved his arms above the desk like a maestro conducting the opera. He was preparing his headline and lead story for the 4th of July celebration edition that was a week off. He didn't look up when the front door opened and Jeb and Janie LaFarge entered the small office. With a few more clicks and a raise of his hands at the song's crescendo, he abruptly removed the needle from the worn 45 in a screeching skip, and lifted his smudged bifocals to his forehead to greet the shabby couple, "Can I be of assistance?"

"Yessiree," Jeb said. "Wez thought it were time sump' 'un was dun 'bout that Co'set fernral home."

Jeb and Janie LaFarge lived in an unkempt boxy house on Poplar Street across from the city park called the Grove. They were certified bohemian dolts in every uneducated, uncombed and undignified manner, receiving both state welfare subsidy and county assistance. Jeb LaFarge carried a tattered letter from the State Of Michigan that declared he was incompetent and proudly displayed it when asked. They, invariably, voiced some sort of self-serving trivial complaint to anyone who would listen.

Pushing himself away from his editor's desk, Scoop Burnham tilted his head sideways in a puzzled look at the disheveled pair, "Just what are you referring too?"

Janie LaFarge stepped forward in one long gangling stride to the edge of Burnham's desk. Standing six-feet tall and dressed in bib overalls, she towered well over the white bushy head of Jeb, and she hovered above the squatty editor. Her cheeks sunk cavernously close to her toothless mouth and transformed her face into a skull like appearance. She spoke in mouthy unintelligent sentences that ended with clenched gums that made her long face shrink half its size. In a deep and manly voice she complained, "We got frenz ats die 'un and dammed if we cain't find out 'bout 'em 'til yer abitchiary comes zout. Wez wunderin' if yous would prent one of them ledders ta the editers fer us. Ya know, tellen 'um to put sump' 'un in the winda in their fernral home say'un whose died." In a quick apologetic sigh with her hand on her forehead she continued; "Jeb un me ain't good at writun', but wez hopun ud write' 'er?" Jeb nodded with Janie. At the center of their concern was the possibility of them missing a free meal. Invariably, after a funeral service the family or church congregation would put on a complimentary meal for funeral attendees at which time the mendicant LaFarges would take advantage of the ritual to get feed. Rarely ever knowing the deceased personally, they would show up uninvited where they satiated their hunger and would leave the funeral feast with their pockets packed with bread rolls, slices of ham and anything else they could carry off.

Scoop smiled in a round grin and looked back at his quiet Underwood and took a moment attempting to decipher the peculiar but familiar vernacular he just witnessed. "Let's see if I've got this right. You would like me to write a letter to the editor, myself, in protest of the Cosette Funeral Home's negligence for not posting the funeral service details of the decedents?"

Jeb and Janie nodded toward each other in puzzled and confused agreement, "Yessiree."

A letter was composed to the editor, by the editor, and signed: Jeb and Janie LaFarge. The letter appeared in that week's edition of the Chandlerville News. From then on a death notice was taped to the bay window of the lobby of the Cosette Funeral Home for all to view. Henceforth, Jeb and Janie were ignobly fed in an uninterrupted frequency.

Jeb and Janie sauntered in a clumsy gate down Main Street retreating to their shabby house on Poplar Street when they saw Chubba Harkins and Clifford Krupp hanging out inside the Grove. "Er aught to be a law ta keep 'em guys outta tha park," Jeb said in a condescending tone.

"When I see Llyod Levin I'm gonna give 'em my piece a mine, that park is fer nice people like us, not them rascalds," Janie declared, "Wez can write another ledders ta the editers-get somp un done 'bout it."

Harkins and Krupp were best friends. Clifford was a muscular seventeen-year-old with summer blond, almost white hair. He was short and cocky and capable of a physical challenge. He and Harkins were good swimmers and often swam the length of Shoepac Lake after swinging and diving from a long rope they tied in the high branches of a Red Pine that hung over the tall banks of the shore. He was athletic and could do graceful one-arm handstands and back flips with ease. He and Chubba complimented each other with their wistful approach to chasing girls at the Curve on Black Lake, and hot rodding old flathead motored cars back and forth through downtown. They often hung out in the Grove, a dense over-grown city park at the end of Main Street where giant soft Maples, and sprawling Elm trees spread themselves in a thick leafy awning. The park benches and picnic tables were whittled with initials carved inside indelicate heart shapes and were feebly masked with layers of green paint in an attempt to obscure them. Chubba was putting the finishing touches on his carving atop a pine board picnic table proclaiming his latest conquest:

I balled Eunice Cummins - C. H.

"Ya bastard," Clifford said as he practiced leaping into a one-arm handstand near the table that Harkins had just carved on. "How long did you have to work on her, couple a months? She's a real babe, too. Lucky you."

"Terri Kellah's next," Chubba said as he brushed away the woodchips from his carving and placed the Buck knife back in his pocket. He stood up and unzipped his blue jeans and began to urinate, "I got the hots foah her, man. Evah see her in that white angora sweatah? I know she wants it bad," he said referring to the large breasted twenty-four year-old high school math teacher, Miss Keller. "If I was a home-ec student I surah would be getting' ah good grade in Eunice's class...Xtrah credit foah aftah school lessons," he laughed with his manhood still exposed though he had finished pissing.

"Done yet?" Clifford inquired as he brushed the blades of grass from his palm.

"With what?"

"Pissin'."

"Wha yeah."

"Then put the horse back in the barn, ya pervert."

"Oh," Harkins replied with a quick stuff and zip.

At the far end of the Grove a trail meandered through a tangle of willows and cottonwood trees and ended at the cement foundations of the Lobdell Emery Steering Wheel Plant. The vast structure had produced most of Detroit's steering wheels from 1901 until it burned to the ground in 1926, but "Chandlerville Steers The World" lingered as the town's motto. Perhaps it had for a time but the fire destroyed all of the immense buildings that comprised its operation and seven workers had perished in the flames, their bodies never recovered. All that remained were the charred concrete walls and deep cement basements that collected rain water in murky pools. A gigantic rusted steel boiler was still intact at the center of the maze with a torched away access door cut into it at one end. The concrete carcass was called the Ruins. There was a foreboding admonition etched into the minds of the town's children by worrisome Chandlerville parents, who told stories of ghosts roaming the concrete skeletal shell. But the old boiler and labyrinth of chest high stone footings had become an enticing playground for bored kids and the occasional discrete hobo passing through town.

Harkins and Krupp brushed back the saplings and shin tangles and entered the Ruins. The concrete walls stood tall and erect with rusted rebar sticking out in places that served as handles to grip when scaling them. The ascent to the top was much easier than the return because climbers had to retreat by feel in their harrowing decent. Harkins and Krupp were very good at it, and were the only ones I knew who had enough guts or stupidity to climb to the crest of the tallest center walls. The four-story structure that was the main portion of the factory stood bleakly grey and towered menacingly above the tree line making it visible all over town. Only one person, Lloyd Marsh, had ever been able to 'walk the wall' which meant walking the entire outline of the top on its jagged and uneven surface. Marsh was a true hero to us by virtue of his 'walk the wall' feat. He made his epic traverse in 1955 during a thunderous rainstorm on a dare from his friends. At the far side of the concrete walls sprung a rusted piece of bent steel reinforcement rod extending six feet above the edge. Hanging from the rod was a tattered and faded red shirt tied in a thick knot where Marsh had placed it in 1955. No one had ever been able to retrieve the shirt as proof of completing the passage. The most heroic and supreme accomplishment anyone could achieve was to complete the death-defying journey and return with the red shirt. Krupp hadn't done it and Harkins hadn't, either.

High on top the center walls Krupp and Harkins sat with their blue jeaned legs straddled across the narrow surface silently pondering the community of Chandlerville below and the small specs of people going about their mundane routine.

"What you going to do next summer after graduation?" Krupp said as he tossed a broken piece of concrete and watched the ripples of dark water splash against the basement walls.

"Prahbly go back to Bahston and live with my Uncle. He can get me ah job at ah shoe factry wheyah he works. You?"

Krupp rose to his feet with toe to heel and his arms away from his sides for balance, "My brother, Paul lives in Alaska and he says there's good money up there. Jobs everywhere, I guess. I know one thing's for sure; I'm gettin' the hell outta Chandlerville."

Far below them a green cluster of high bush cranberries mysteriously rustled in a stiff breeze as though someone had sneaked through them. The boys glanced down toward the disturbance and shrugged.

"I'm gonna walk the wall," Krupp whispered as he stared over to the red shirt where it hung precariously elevated from the wall.

"You shittin'?"

"Nah, I'm not," he said and slid his foot forward and then the next until he was far away from the dropped jaw of Chubba Harkins. "Half way there," Clifford's voice echoed off the hard walls.

"Okay, that's fah enough ya' asshole!" Harkins yelled.

"Shit man, this is easy."

"Now come on, you don't have ta prove anything ta me," Harkins spoke in great concern and he raised himself to his feet and watched closely at Krupp's steps wishing he could guide them. Krupp continued along the treacherous wall with his arms raised from his sides until he was nearly to the steel bar that held the red shirt. Beneath his feet small pebbles broke away from the brittle concrete and fell into the black water below. He looked down in time to watch them create tiny ringlets on the water's surface. Far across the wide opening the boys looked toward each other in apprehensive silence.

"A few more…" Krupp hollered. Through his mind sped the visions of applause and adulation he would receive when he hoisted the red shirt for the entire town to see. He saw himself sitting upon a joyous float that would crawl along the crowded Main Street in the 4th of July parade that was coming the next week. Autographs and impromptu photographs would follow him for the rest of his days in Chandlerville. There would be a statue in his likeness erected next to Emmitt Chandler's. As he took his final step toward the red shirt a brisk wind gathered and sang across the apex of the walls and knocked him off balance. His head turned quickly and he grabbed at his cheek as though a bee had stung him. A large piece of concrete broke away from his footing and he began to fall. In a frantic grab he was able to clutch and hold onto the fragile wall. His legs and feet kicked wildly searching for a foothold. Clifford Krupp clung desperately to the crumbling surface and the vines of ivy that had grown to the top. He felt the wall give way. He and a large piece of foundation plummeted to the shallow black water below. His scream echoed inside the vacuum of the foundation walls. Chubba Harkins' silhouette stood minute and vague against the western sky and his doleful cry was swallowed in obscurity across the Ruins onto the deaf Chandlerville streets below.

Chapter 12
Dancing Ghosts

"That's it, just slide the cover off," Willie said as the wooden top came loose in my hands; "Easy now, gently."

"I got it," I said while bending deep inside the dark hole as the brown damp sticks came into view where they laid neatly in stacked rows within the box. We sat with fixed stares above the opening and pondered what to do next.

"Lift one out but be very careful," Verdi warned. I cautiously placed a couple of fingers and thumb along the top row of damp sticks and lifted one out of the box. Hesitantly, I displayed the cylinder and the boys retreated on their rumps to what they thought was a safe distance away from me. "Lemme have it," a bright-eyed Verdie asked with an outstretched hand. "Get the fuse, now." The rest of the boys regained their courage and huddled next to Verdie and the moist stick was gently passed back and forth like a shared cigarette.

"Look at that," Denis said as he examined the simple design; "It feels kinda wet."

"Wondah if it still works?" A doubting Johnny said when he handed it to Willie. "It looks like a giant firecrackah."

"It is a giant firecracker!" Willie exclaimed while examining both ends of the stick. "See there," he pointed at the end of the stick, "That's where the fuse goes...either end."

I reached inside the hole and removed the spiral cord of blasting fuse and set it on the floor, "Let's try it."

"I saw how it was done on The Lone Ranger, once," Denis offered.

"Yeah? How's that?" The skeptical Willie asked.

"Well..." Denis paused.

"I think it's kinda obvious what has ta be done. We got ta shove a piece of that blasting cord into one end of the stick, the longer the piece the more time we have to get the hell outta the way," Willie said as he studied the dynamite stick and the curled spool of cord.

It was decided that the river would be the safest place to ignite the 'giant firecracker'. So we marched from the shack with the dynamite and cord but hesitated on the porch to let our eyes adjust to the blinding late afternoon sunlight. A cool refreshing breeze carried from the river across our blushed faces and dried the sweat on our foreheads. We assembled at the river's edge and Willie cut a foot long piece of cord from the spool and tediously wrapped it around the brown dynamite cylinder and tied it in a knot. The river swept by in a churning and black swirling flow and we looked at each other as though we were waiting for a recess bell to ring so we could launch ourselves to safety once the fuse was lit.

"Match," Willie shouted.

"Got one," Verdie nervously retrieved an Ohio Blue Tip and handed it to Willie. The rest of us slowly eased from the riverbank until only Willie and Verdie remained.

"Here goes..." Willie warned and dragged the match head against his bent leg and taught blue jean thigh where it erupted in a yellow blue flame. The grey fused smoldered for a moment above the match flame and began to burn toward the awaiting dynamite. In a long toss above the river the dynamite cart wheeled end over end until it plashed into the fast water. We dashed frantically for cover through the thick swale grass when Johnny Harkins fell into the yellow brown tangle. The fleeting Verdie and Willie lifted him to his feet and we hid behind the shack and waited for the explosion. Like watching a pot of water sitting on an open flame trying to boil we waited, and waited until it was undeniably certain that nothing was going to happen; no deafening boom, no 'whump' of water shooting skyward. Nothing.

The sun began to lower across the western sky and the shack became flooded with shade inside the swamp and behind the muted tree line. Near the river the remains of a stone lined fire pit was cleared away and we broke dead limbs from cedar trees to make a fire. Denis and Johnny stood at the bank and casted upstream and reeled their red and white dare devils back to the shore. Our brown knapsacks lay by the fire, and opened bindles were spread out like haphazard picnic fare. Verdie and Willie, in a slow and guarded walk, returned from the shack holding their knapsacks across their chests and placed them gently upon the springy grass away from the fire.

"Don't go near these," Willie said and everyone looked toward him. Inside the sacks they had placed a dozen wet sticks of dynamite wrapped in the old newspapers that had lain on the floor of shack. They weren't finished yet with their quest to ignite the explosives. I opened a couple cans of beans and placed them near the edge of the flickering flames and spread my blue wool blanket across a cushion of swale grass near the pit and sat on it. No one spoke, but I knew we were all thinking about the dynamite and how it let us down.

"Decent," Johnny complimented while Denis fought with his bent Shakespeare pole that held a long and plump Northern Pike at the end of his line. He held the slimy eight-pound jack for us to view and tossed it on the bank; "Dinner."

"More dinner," Johnny added while reeling in another jack he caught on a cluster of crawlers and a #9 snelled hook. Soon there was enough fish for all of us and we kneeled by the river and cleaned them with dull knives. Just a slit on their under belly and a handful of entrails, then a dip into the stream and they were ready for a sapling skewer held over an open flame.

The light of the flames bounced faintly off the shack like dancing ghosts as we crouched by the pit turning the pieces of salted jack fillets close to the fire. A loaf of Mom's bread toasted deliciously on aluminum foil close to the embers and we tore away jagged steaming chunks with our fish scented hands to dip into the bubbling bean broth. I brushed away a drip of broth from my chin and thought to myself; there is no meal so good as the quenching of a famished hunger at a fireside feast when eyes, nose and mouth come together in a powerful marriage. This could only take place on a summer's riverbank with crickets singing and nighthawks zooming overhead on the sills of the evening.

We sat close to the orange embers and felt its radiant flush washing our faces. We were warm, comfortable and satisfied. A distant bugle of an elk sang through the dense swamp and we paid little attention to it. We were in the wilderness now where the cover of the night brought mysterious sounds of branches breaking, leaves rustling and cries from yipping coyote packs calling to help in a kill. Later, the sound of nothing rung in our ears; we begged for a familiar sound as we jostled about near the dying fire to find a comfortable position during the doldrums of the night.

Willie rose from his sleeping bag in a sudden epiphany, "What is dynamite made of? Nitroglycerin! That's why it didn't explode." By this time Verdie was sitting up and swiped at the twisted knot of hair bristling from his head, "What are you talking about?"

"Nitroglycerin will not ignite if it's wet. Basic chemistry, Verdie."

"Oh yeah, now I remember. Water diffuses the catalyst and renders the cellulose nitrate agent neutral. Ha, ha!"

"What else was missing, Verdie?" Verdie pawed at the unruly hair sprouting on his head. "Don't tell me. Wait a minute..."

"There has to be ignition," Willie anxiously replied with the answer; "Nitro is unstable, it has to have an explosion occur to set it off. I think there has to be a blasting cap attached to it."

By this time all of us were sitting upright and listening to the chemistry kids figuring out the problem. The riddle of the dud was going to be solved.

"I didn't see anything else in the hole, did you?" Willie asked in case there may have been blasting caps lying beside the box. Verdie and I shook our heads.

"We'll get it to work, my friends."

Denis churned the coals of the fading fire with a stick and brought it back to life as sparks carried off into the dark and made the tin roof of the shack shimmer like ghosts dancing in a sparkling parade.

A bullfrog groaned near the river and I lifted my head from the blue blanket to see a deer leap back into the thick cover of the cedar swamp.

The morning dampness coated our clothes and our fishing poles where they laid in the swale. Everything around the campsite dripped in morning moisture and we wiped the night from our faces with our forearms. The sunrise had begun much earlier but hadn't crested the cedars to spray its warmth on us. The fire had gone out and we had become chilled by its absence. We hurried about the camp and gathered our gear to return home. The ultimate joy one could receive was always the planning, preparation and participation in the journey but the second most delightful part was getting back home. But, back home the grim funeral home business was being carried out.

Chapter 13
Heart Break and Spun Yarn

Pa parked the long blue Ford hearse in the alley next to the side door that lead to the embalming room. Inside the hearse's long tunnel Clifford Krupp lay broken on the gurney and was covered with a white linen sheet. He had just returned from recovering the body from the basement of the Ruins. He had spent most of the night with the State Police, County Sheriff and Lloyd Levin trying to get to and remove Krupp through the barrier of overgrowth engulfing the spot where he had died. He was exhausted and paused to lean on the fender of the hearse. Mom stepped from the alley door, "You look beat," she said as she placed her hand on his shoulder.

"If ever I needed da boys to help was last night. You wouldn't believe how hard it was getting him out a dat dungeon."

"It musta been. You've been out there all night, Romeo."

"We had to haul da gurney a half mile back threw da tickest brush and over dose concrete walls. Tank God da police were dare ta help."

Mom stood close to the undertaker and rubbed his shoulders before she asked, "Was Fritz there?" There was a pause before he answered.

"No, but Lloyd went to his house an told him. I dread seeing him."

Fritz Krupp was Clifford's father and my father's best friend in Chandlerville. The two spent hours drinking countless bottles of beer holding endless discussions on any topic that came to mind. Fritz was mesmerizing with his eloquent colloquial speech and a prolific storyteller. He could hold a listener captive with his vivid descriptions and velvety smooth delivery through his whiskey and beer stained voice. He worked by himself cutting poplar bolts called 'short wood' and delivered them in his battered Ford Stake truck to Buza Saw Mill where they were made into pallets. His gnarled knuckles on his worn out hands displayed a history of deep wounds from the slaps of logging chains, the crushing of misguided cinch handles and violent smashes of rolling logs. A chainsaw had claimed a finger on his left hand and a dozer track took another from his right. But his blue gray eyes peered contently and intelligently below heavy eyelids and above a salt and pepper beard.

The body of Clifford Krupp now lay on the cold porcelain table in the embalming room. Pa slid his arms into a white lab coat and buttoned it closed across his chest. The door opened slowly and Mom entered. "Fritz is here, Romeo. He wants to see his son."

Pa leaned on one hand against a narrow counter and took a breath to prepare for what he knew would be the hardest part of being an undertaker. The years of night schooling he took and the hours of studying he did after a long days shift as a tool and die man would have to take over now. The courses in family bereavement hardly were enough to shield his heart from the heaviness that came when dealing with death, especially the death of a best friend's son.

Fritz Krupp entered the room and looked down where his son lay on the white table. The two men stepped toward each other and my father took the venerable hands of his friend and held them tightly in his. They stood in quite grief trying to hold back the welling of sorrow but like a thunderstorm that gathers and eventually explodes the men broke past the thin barrier of composure and wept.

Fritz stepped to the side of the table and removed the linen sheet with his trembling disfigured hand. The boy's face was swollen nearly beyond recognition from the blood that erupted within his body when he struck the ground. On the side of his cheek was small raised welt. "My beautiful son. He was going to be my legacy, Romeo. The son every father wants born to him. Look at what he is now... look how the life has drained from him," he continued through quick sobbing breathes while reminiscing, "When he was a baby his legs were bowed and the doctors wanted to put him in casts to straighten them, I said no. I knew what had to be done," Fritz said as he placed his hands on Clifford's leg; "So every day, for hours at a time, I would rub them and shape them and hold him when he cried. I saw strength in his small blue eyes and he seemed to know what I was trying to do, even though it was painful and hurting but soon his legs began to straighten and..." Fritz Krupp placed his head on his son's chest and a flood of tears dampened the boy's shirt. He looked up at Pa through his once content blue grey eyes and begged, "Make him beautiful again, Romeo. Make him beautiful again for his mother."

The undertaker stepped quietly from the embalming room past the heavy blue curtains that hung from the ceiling. He knew his friend needed to be alone with his son for the last time.

Chapter 14
The Reenactment

    Our final ride dropped Willie off at his house on M-68 and he lifted himself off Cal Madden's hay wagon and brushed the chaff from his jeans. We were tired, hungry and happy to return to town. It was near noon and the trip back to Chandlerville took hours with intermittent rides and exhaustive hiking in the hazy morning heat. "Remember, guys, don't say a word to anyone. If they catch us with this stuff we're in deep shit." He clutched the bag holding six dynamite sticks to his chest and walked up the driveway to his house. We rode on the rickety tractor-pulled wagon up town and got off by the funeral home in time to see Fritz Krupp leaving and drive off in his Ford truck.

    Behind the funeral home a square white paint-peeling garage with double swinging doors was dark when we went inside. Our eyes adjusted and we kneeled in a circle around the knapsack Verdie laid on the concrete floor. He unwrapped the sticks from the newspapers and placed them in a row. The sticks were warm to the touch and had begun to dry out during our return home. A wet slippery residue had collected on their bottoms and Verdie wiped some of it from his hand on the edge of a nearby work counter. "We got ta find a good hiding place. Can't put it in here, Pa might find it."

"What abat tha foart?" Johnny asked.

"If it gets raided by Pratt then they'll find it. Can't imagine what would happen if they got their grubs on it, ay?" He paused and placed his chin on his sweaty open palm and began to ponder. There were countless places to hide the goods, innumerable nooks and compartments everywhere we looked in the dim garage. He thought of the coal bin in the basement, no. The narrow floor joist openings in the same area, no. Perhaps dig a deep hole in the field where the fort sat, no. Finally, he stood up, "I know just the place," and he began rewrapping the oozing sticks in the newspapers. "Yous guys check out the fort and make sure everything is decent and I'll meet you there in a few minutes." We departed the warm garage in different directions but soon would meet at the fort.

Froggy and Craig were waiting inside when we got there. They pounded us like targets in a shooting range with a myriad of questions and begged for a reenactment of our trip. We held them off as best we could until Verdie arrived because Johnny and I had rounds of anxious questions of our own to fire off.

"Were'd ya hide it, Verdie?" I asked in anticipation. Verdie smiled and pulled up a bucket and sat down.

"Come on; tell us what tha hell happened. Did yous find dynamite? Did ya light it? Come on," Craig begged.

"Yeah, don't keep us waitin', damn," Froggy said in a restless posture.

"Ay," the voice said on the outside of the burlap door and Willie ducted inside. We were all present now and the story of the wild trip began from Curly Bowman's glorious ash that hung defiantly from his homemade cigarette, to Macey Maserone's benevolent lift out to the 'crock in the road'.

"It was a hellova time, I didn't think I could walk anymore when we got to the bridge. My legs felt like lead," I said as we began our slightly embellished recitation.

"Yeah, the shack was right where I said, wasn't it?" Willie said hoping for praise.

"When we got inside the shack and there was nothing there I was thinkin', man, this is bullshit," Denis added. "Leave it ta Chris, he's a real snooper. He found a secret spot in the floor and opened it and there it was..."

I beamed in a broad smile and Craig slapped me on the back.

"Was this where ya found it?" Froggy said with raised eyebrows. We looked at him in slight disbelief and Denis gave him a poke to his ribs. "Then what happened?"

I took over and began to spin out my version of the discovery. I knew I could have complete poetic freedom because the story would be much better than if someone else from the group told it. And, I thought to myself, who's going to challenge its accuracy when I make them look like heroes in the end. But before then I was going to glorify myself.

"Yeah, these assholes gave up on it. 'There ain't no dynamite', they said. I knew better, though. Yep. They all left the shack and I started kickin' 'round on the floor and suddenly I see this 'coon hidin' in the corner behind a bunch a trash. We looked at each other and he growls and flashes his teeth at me. I didn't back away, though. We just stared each other down until he turned and scurried out the hole he came from." Willie, Verdie, Denis and Johnny looked at me and turned their heads away in embarrassed smiles. "Well I see this table in the corner and I noticed a hole drilled into the floor. It's a trap door but when I tried to lift it, it wouldn't budge. So Willie and Verdie says, 'There ain't nothin' there,' and I says watch this. I pulled real hard and it still wouldn't come apart, but Willie and Verdie grabs at it and 'pop', it comes free. We look down the hole but we can't see shit 'cause it's way too dark. I says to Denis, 'gimme a candle and yous guys hold my feet and I'll dangle in the hole ta see what's there,'" Froggy and Craig inched closer to me like kids hearing a glorious bedtime story. The other witness' leaned back and enjoyed the colorful recollection.

"Go on," Willie said enjoying the yarn with his spindly forearms crossed on his chest.

"Yeah, come on. What happened next?" Denis said while becoming engulfed in my spin.

"Okay, deep in the hole I see this wooden box but I'll be damned there's a bunch a rats scurrying around like ants. I got ta get to the box so I holds the candle at 'em and they're afraid of the light, their eyes were white as the sky and their teeth were long as railroad spikes. Finally, they get the hell outa the way and Willie says, 'lift the cover on the box but be easy with it,' he says, but hell, I know that. I get the cover off and grabs a couple sticks and they begin to pull me up. Damned if I didn't drop one. But I grabs it just in time before it hits the other sticks, that woulda been a disaster, ay?"

I went on and on in great detail of how Denis and Johnny saved the day with the eight-pound jacks they caught that were now twelve pounds and how we would have starved if it weren't for them. And how brave Verdie and Willie were when they stood alone at the riverbank lighting the dynamite that could have blown them to smithereens. I described a wonderful but fictitious scene where they rescued Johnny when he became entangled in the swale and couldn't break free until they hauled him behind the shack just as the dynamite exploded in the river and rained down pieces of slimy jacks and flopping brook trout.

"Wow. Twelve pounds?" Froggy said in amazement.

"God, I wish I was there with yous," lamented Craig.

We sat inside the fort and rehashed the story in great length with laughs and plans of what to do with the remaining dynamite sticks. There was the idea of launching an old car into the sky down at the junkyard behind the Marathon Gas Station, maybe blow up the old boiler in the Ruins. Our minds melded together like pages in a novel that led to an exciting ending until Craig asked, "Someone die?"

"Why's that?" Verdie asked.

"Been cars comin' and goin' at yer place all mornin', and Lloyd Levin's was there, too."

We recalled seeing Fritz Krupp leaving the funeral home and, suddenly, we wondered if it had anything to do with him. We hadn't seen Pa or Mom since we returned so we didn't know that there had been a call. We didn't know about Clifford Krupp, yet.

"Remember," Willie shouted for our attention, "Loose lips sink ships," We waved in agreement as we departed the fort.

Chapter 15
The Dregs of Presque Isle

We brothers trudged up the steep back stairwell that led to the enclosed porch where Mom was feeding wet clothes into the ringer of a Maytag washing machine. Damp shirts, pants and dingy socks sat in a pile inside a basket waiting to be hung on the backyard clotheslines.

"You're back," Mom said surprised. "Did yous have a good time? How was the fishin'?" Mom asked before she began to tell us of the Clifford Krupp call.

"It was a good trip and we caught some decent fish," Verdie said when it was his turn to give Mom a hug.

"I caught a twelve pounder, Mom. Shoulda seen it," Denis recalled from a new memory of our trip.

"We get a call?" I asked. Mom flipped the switch of the Maytag and began to tell us about Clifford.

"They were trying to walk the walls of the Ruins and something happened when Clifford tried to get some damned red shirt. Young Harkins said it looked like he was pushed from the wall but there wasn't anyone else with 'em. He swears someone or something shoved Clifford off balance but I don't know how that could be." In a stern finger pointing she continued, "yous better not ever go there. I better not ever hear yous are going to them damned Ruins or there'll be trouble from me," she said and pulled us together in a group hug. "It's no place for kids, nothin' but evil things down there."

We marched to our bedroom in heavy weary steps from our exhausting morning, and I climbed to my top bunk where my head collapsed onto a comfortable pillow. Verdie and Denis took their places and stretched out on the neatly made beds. Nothing was said but we recalled memories of Clifford Krupp and imagined the horrible fall he took. We were becoming calloused to the reality that death could come at any time to anyone, but today we were secretly thankful it was someone else and not one of us. We were saddened about Clifford's demise, but secretly glad that the red shirt still remained on the wall. Mom opened the door to our room and whispered, "Don't forget, yous are serving mass tonight." We fell into a comfortable sleep atop our neatly made beds.

Far too soon, Mom's gentle knock on the door awakened us. "Time to go, boys. I've got your cassocks ready." We rolled off the beds and made ready for mass. We piled into the Bellaire station wagon and Verdie called "shotgun" so Denis and I sat on the back seat. Mom dropped us off behind the church. When we entered the church's sacristy Father Klein, dressed in his white alb, was placing hosts into the chalice. Hanging from the honey colored oak paneled walls were bright green, gold, and purple chasubles that were lined with gold and silver accoutrements worn to transform the priest into a heavenly and splendorous appearance. We began to pull the long black cassocks over our heads and tugged them into place where they hung long to the floor. We were getting bored of being altar boys and wished we could quit, but Mom would be devastated if we did. There had to be a way of getting out of the chore that seemed to interrupt our Saturdays and Sundays. There were other altar boys and we weren't expected to serve every weekend but when it was our turn it was annoyingly inconvenient.

Father Klein placed the chalice on a cloth-covered counter and turned to us with a barrage of interrogations and insults. There were times when he could be an indignant prick and today was one of them. "Let's get it right today, damnit," he looked toward Denis and singled him out. "You are the worst one, Denis. Have you learned your Latin responses correctly? I will not stand for another mistake during mass. There's no excuse for it. You DO have your lesson book at home, don't you?" he said in a mean and acrimonious voice. This wasn't the first time we heard him swear so we weren't surprised. We nodded with our heads lowered. Glenn Cavanaugh, another altar boy was dressing in the far corner of the room and didn't say anything while the priest chewed on us. Glenn Cavanaugh was a shy eleven-year old whose doting parents, unflatteringly, called 'Lamb'. Like us, Lamb was forced into altar boy servitude by well-meaning parents. He was impressionable and watched us carefully as his Latin and altar routine was a notch below ours. Father Klein reached for the green chasuble on the wall and put it on. He adjusted the white stole over his shoulders to finish his dress, and we proceeded through the door that led to the ornate altar and the awaiting congregation.

Verdie and I were of a temperament where we could adjust to an ass chewing and we let it roll out of our minds with ease, but not Denis. We could tell that the priest's lecture was bothering him when his chin lowered and a twisted sneer came over his squinting eyes and clenched teeth. We followed the reverent priest while he swung the smoldering incense thurible back and forth on its chain and we genuflected as we crossed the altar to take our positions for mass. There was another thurible smoking in Denis' mind and Verdie and I knew that he was going to do something, probably something outrageous.

"Et cum spi rit u tuo," Father Klein recited. Verdie and I responded with a sign of the cross. Father Klein's face skewed and Denis, whose face had become red with anger, held his clenched fists hidden behind his cassock. Slowly he began swallowing copious gulps of air. Verdie and I heard the sounds of his slurping slugs and, raising our eyebrows thought, 'oh no'. Just when we felt he could swallow no more he took one final enormous swig of air. It was time for a Latin response so Denis took over. Throughout the echoing walls of the church came a diatribe of incoherent backwards verbiage that fell unscrupulously on all ears delivered in the tune of the hit song, 'Monster Mash,' and a familiar choreography we had seen before. Verdie, thinking 'oh what the hell' began to clap out the rhythm of the beat and I joined in.

Clap...clap, clap. Clap...clap, clap. Denis fed off of our in-time cadence and delivered his recital of gibberish to the corresponding clapping beats. A confounded congregation raised their heads in fear as though the devil himself had taken over mass. Signs of the cross were protectively made and Father Klein bristled in acute anger as we carried out the vengeful presentation. Glenn Cavanaugh, feebly trying to contain his uncontrollable laugh, failed, and the front of his cassock showed the results of his weak bladder and urine pooled around his feet. Father Klein, in a controlled rage ordered us from the altar, and we obliged in unsuppressed mirth. Glenn Cavanaugh, in a frighten flight, tripped on his 'too long' cassock and sprawled across the marble floor like a fallen saint, adding to the slapstick hilarity of the scene. By now, the congregation had become an audience that came to the conclusion that Satan wasn't speaking from the altar, so they erupted in broad laughter and the church filled with loud 'har har's' and ardent uproarious squeals. An agitated and furious priest turned to the congregation and declared, "the mass will now end, go in peace."

In our rapid departure from the sacristy, cassocks were swiftly hurled to the floor as we bolted through the door and fled for the safety of the fort. Behind us, we heard the echoes of Father Klein's screams carry over the church lawn, "Blasphemy! Blasphemy! You're nothing but dregs, dregs of the county. Dregs of Presque Isle."

We flipped open the burlap and hurled ourselves inside the quiet of the fort and slapped our knees in raucous laughter, "I can't believe you did that, Denis. What a show," Verdie sighed as our broad smiles relaxed.

"Think we'll be serving mass anytime soon?" I chuckled.

"I guess I showed that asshole priest I been practicing my Latin," Denis added while leaning back on his bucket in total gratification. "That was the best I've ever done," he shined while letting out the remaining burps, "What did he call us?"

I smiled, "Dregs. Dregs of Presque Isle," I thought for a moment, "I like that. The Dregs of Presque Isle, it has a nice ring to it."

"What the hell is a dreg?" Verdie asked.

"Can't be anything good in Father Klein's mind," I concluded.

We ended our procrastination of returning home, because we knew we would face another form of music; Mom. So we made way through the thickly weeded field heading for home.

"You do the talkin'," Verdie instructed when he looked at me. We hardly had a defense to our actions, but if there were any hope in a lesser punishment it would have to come by me. He knew that if I was the spokesman for the group Mom would center her verbal reaming toward me and not him, besides, he had faith in my quick thinking and quintessential ability to deliver bullshit on the spot. I quickly composed a hasty defense and told my brothers, "I'll do the explainin'."

"Decent."

We entered the living room just as Mom was hanging up the phone. Without asking, we knew it was Father Klein delivering the bad report. In our mother's eyes a priest was held in the highest esteem. They could do no wrong because they were anointed the 'voice of God'. Having been raised in a strict Irish Catholic household, religion and faith in the church were ingrained and proselytized in her from childhood. Her most glorious dream was for one of us to become an ordained priest. She picked me for that position. Every so often, she would recall how she had trouble carrying me through her difficult pregnancy and how Grand Pere Cosette, who was a doctor, had told her I wasn't to be born. But she prayed with a vigilant dedication and made a promise to Christ that if He would grant her my birth she would name me after Him and Saint Christopher, the patron saint of travelers. In her mind, I was the obvious choice for priesthood but I felt and acted in no such way.

We collected in a humble assembly in front of Mom and waited for her to begin her onslaught. At the very least, our punishment would be the loss of our 4th of July privileges and the handsome allowance we would have received. She stood with her arms folded across her blue apron and examined each of us through narrowed eyes before she spoke, "Well, you've really dunnit now, haven't you?"

"That was Father Klein on the phone, wasn't it?" I asked meekly confident of the answer.

"Yes, he said you boys put on a memorable performance during mass tonight."

"He did?"

"Especially Denis. Oh, I wish I was there to see it," she exclaimed. "My boys putting on another performance for all of the church congregation to see."

Apparently, after our blazing departure, Father Klein did his customary stroll through the center aisle where he was met with applause and adulation from the approving audience. They thought that Denis' impromptu enactment of 'Monster Mash' was rehearsed and intentional. The priest was complimented with firm handshakes and pats on the back from the appreciative congregation where he stood outside of the church entrance. "That was one of the best masses I've ever attended, Father," Raymond Beauregard declared.

"I'd like to see this more often," Irene Booth requested then apologetically whispered; "truth be told, mass can get a little boring at times, Father, but this was wonderful." Father Klein's palliated anger turned to prideful smiles as he accepted the gracious compliments from the adorning churchgoers while taking full credit for the event.

"Oh, and Father said he'd like to see yous next week in the rectory. Now, let's get ready for dinner."

We retreated to our bedroom in bittersweet relief having avoided harsh reprisal but failing to be rid of our altar boy duties.

Chapter 16
The New Member

Dozens of freshly washed cars were parked in an orderly line along Main Street in front of the funeral home and beyond Leed's Grocery Store; Fay's Clothing and extended into another block to the front of the Dairy Queen. Verdie, Denis and I hurried to place magnetic funeral flags on their fenders before the procession began. Clifford Krupp lay wrapped in the pillow lining of a bronze casket where it rested on a bier. Fritz and Evelyn Krupp sat holding each other in mourning on a long blue couch facing the casket and dozens of flower arrangements. Fritz looked out of character in his black suit. We had never seen him in a suit. He was always dressed for the woods; heavy cotton pants held up with suspenders stretched over a flannel shirt and weathered high-top Red Wings laced half way up. A colorful wool chapeau forever sat tilted and dignified on his grey hair but not today. A morose funeral hymn scratched out a mournful melody of 'Nearer My God To Thee' on the thirty-three and a third player in the back of the chapel. Reverend Berger finished his brief sermon and the attendees lined up to console the Krupps and pay final respects to Clifford when they passed by his casket. We waited by the side doors that led to the alley where the polished blue Ford hearse was parked glowing in the ten-o'clock shade. Chubba Harkins and the rest of the pallbearers wearing funeral faces wheeled the bier and casket through the now empty chapel into the alley and lifted it into the back of the hearse. Fritz stood alone beside the hearse and was fraught with tears. He stepped further away from the group and broke down in a flood of anguish. I edged up and stood beside him wanting to put a succored hand on his shoulder and cry in condolence but didn't. Before tears began to well up I remembered how Pa had warned us to keep our feelings inside and be professional, no matter whom it was. I obeyed but wish I hadn't. Fritz reached over and took my hand, "Thank you, son," acknowledging my hesitant gesture. He knew Pa's rule, too, but understood.

  The funeral procession slowly drove down Main Street in a long stream of cars, past the Midway Diner where complacent customers holding coffee cups peered through the window. The procession ended at Edgewood Cemetery where Clifford was lowered six feet into the ground and covered with earth.

  Our work was nearly done. It was our responsibility to clean the chapel and dispose of the remaining flowers, fold and stack the dozens of chairs and sweep and tidy the chapel. We didn't need any Roman helmets, we had a stack of them, and so we threw the flowerpots next to the burn barrel in the alley. Through the front bay window we could see Jeb and Janie LaFarge studying the notice taped to the glass trying to decipher the name of the deceased and, more importantly, find out where the funeral luncheon would be held.

  Finally, the late June arid sky began collecting rain clouds and was darkening to the west. We headed for the fort and a light rain began to fall. Inside, we could see lighting brighten the walls with quick flashes and we counted the seconds until we heard the thunder. We figured the storm was in Tower and heading our way fast. I curled the burlap back on the fort's opening and there stood Lamb Cavanaugh in the pelting rain. His white tee shirt and pants were soaked more than what the new rain could have done and he was crying, "What's wrong?" I asked but he couldn't break from his sobs. "Come on in;" and I pulled up a bucket for him to sit on. His round face was dotted with brown freckles and his blue eyes were bright and slightly bulging. There was a prominent blue scar below his chin that looked like it was left there from some hasty surgery that had gone wrong. He was eleven-years old and skinny as a slice of bacon. His father, Eldon, like many fathers from town, worked on the Carl D. Bremen, an ore freighter that sailed out of Calcite City. Being dedicated to his job, he spent most of the nine months of the sailing season plowing around the Great Lakes hauling ore and limestone to steel mills in Chicago, Cleveland, Detroit and out to Tonawanda, New York. An ore freighter sailor's life was a lonely one. The money was good, but a man's family life sometimes paid a price. Between intermittent bawling he began to tell us what had happened.

"I was... huh, huh, cutting through the alley behind the Post Office," he stammered with couple more sobs, "to drop some mail for my Mom, huh, huh, and Pratt and his gang cornered me." He started to collect himself now and was able to tell us without tearful interruptions, "they asked me if I had any money, I told 'em no. But they didn't believe me and pulled my pockets inside out." His voice was now getting stronger and was changing to anger. "They stood in a circle and pushed me back and forth like a pinball, then they threw me down on the gravel and stood in a circle and pissed on me." He brushed away the remaining tears and took a seat on the bucket. We brothers looked at each other with stiff faces and shook our heads. Verdie spoke, "They are sonzabitches, we know, but why did ya come here?"

Lamb, with his head hung low to his piss soaked shirt, lifted his bulging eyes and replied, "I wanna' join yous guys at the fort."

Verdie leaned back in surprise. Denis and I looked at each with tilted heads and a long silence dragged out. Finally, we huddled in a quick convening and I told Lamb to step from the fort so we could talk. By now the rain was coming down in pelting sheets and was collecting in a clay-stained pool by the entrance. Obediently, Lamb slipped into the downpour and stood like a sentinel outside the burlap door. We could have felt bad for making him leave but he needed a good soaking to rinse the piss from his clothes. A bold decision would have to be made: Should we allow another person to join our esoteric fort or not? We decided that it was going to take a group vote to induct a new member. We would have to collect all of the members together just to see if there was room enough in the stingy confines of the fort. We sent Lamb Cavanaugh on his way but told him to meet us at ten-o'clock the next morning.

The thunderstorm had passed through the night with a good soaking and left shallow puddles scattered in the alleys and thirsty fields. The farmers were happy knowing the corn, once again, would meet the benchmark of being knee high by the 4th of July. The members of the fort were all present and pulled up in a tight circle. Denis took the floor and like a Grand Poobah of a clandestine monarchy, placed a Roman helmet on his head, and held a dried cattail spear in his hand to replete his exultation. "Let the meeting come to order," he declared. He looked like a haphazardly adorned jungle king from a far off land and we rocked on our buckets and chairs in uncontained laugher. He let out a snort and tossed the helmet and spear into the corner, "Okay, okay," and once again he gained our attention. "Seems there's been a guy..." he stammered momentarily, "you tell 'em, Chris."

I rose, and began to tell the group about the membership application. I had thought about it overnight and slowly warmed up to Lamb's request for admission and my presentation would reflect that. "Boys. Here's what's happened. Seems the Frenchtown gang has done it again but this time they crossed the line. You guys know Lamb Cavanaugh?"

"Yeah, isn't he that little kid with the scar?" Willie replied.

"Yup, one and only. Little kid is right. Helpless. Pratt an' his assholes did a terrible thing, they roughed him up for money and when they didn't get any they pushed him to the ground and pissed all over him, just like he was a patch a nothin'. Well, Lamb shows up here and he's cryin' and drenched in piss."

"Why'd he come heah?" Johnny asked.

"He's so small, man. That's just not right," added Craig.

"That's what I'm gettin' at. He wants ta join the fort." I paused while they thought about it. "Look, his ol' man's on the boats and he doesn't see him hardly 'atall. There's no one to look out for 'em."

"Well, what ya think he can add if he's a member, hell, he ain't no bigger than a flea?" Verdie argued.

"He's got some sand," I replied, "'member when I told him to wait outside while we talked and the thunder and lightning was crashin' all around, and it was rainin' cats n dogs?"

"Yeah, it was," Verdie recalled, "he didn't budge from that spot, did he? That's say's sump'un about 'em. Tough little shit."

"He's got my vote," Froggy declared.

"What the hell, why not," Craig voted, and soon the entire group was in agreement.

"There's got to be an initiation test, guys," Willie reasoned. "He's too small to be an asset in a rumble, hell; we'd have to be watchin' over him like a little brother."

I looked around the circle of heads slightly worried that they felt that way about me but Willie gave me a reassuring look and continued, "He could be of some use in a pinch, though. But, I think he should pass some test to get in."

A confluence of cacophonous conversations collided and erupted into a raucous rumble of suggestions, some of which were as disgusting as the punishment that led Lamb Cavanaugh to seek our harbor of protection. Suddenly, I remembered my entrance exam and blurted above the noise, "Wait, wait, everyone. I think I've got it," All voices ceased and I said, "What about the can of teeth?" The members of the fort smiled and giggled gleefully with the suggestion of the 'can of teeth'. Oh, what a superb test it would be and the quorum agreed.

In the embalming room, high on a shelf, sat a tall New Era Potato Chips can brimming with false teeth. The teeth were a collection of stained, yellowed dentures that either didn't fit right, or made the deceased's face look puffy or bulging. My father would opt to staple their jaws together with stainless steel wire driven into each gum. Then he would tightly twist the wires together to keep their mouths closed. He used cotton to fill the voids in their mouths. The leftover dentures were tossed into the New Era Potato Chips can. Denis sneaked into the embalming room through the alley door and made off with the can of teeth and returned to the fort. It was close to ten-o'clock and Lamb would be arriving soon. We placed the can of teeth on a bucket in the center of our gathering and sifted through the discolored, putrid prosthetics with acrid faces. There were large toothy top plates and ground down bottom ones with yellow tarter collected between the stained rows revealing bits and pieces of food; perhaps, remnants of meals that were their last. Denis pawed through the top layer, and lying inside was a dull grey glass eyeball. He held it up and pointed the lifeless orb at us as though it were an eerie beacon atop a Cyclops's lighthouse. "I'll keep an eye out for yous." We laughed and begged to hold it, but he stuffed it into the safety of his blue jean pocket. The door flap was turned back and Lamb politely asked to enter the fort. We turned and faced the hopeful applicant with stern, examining eyes and motioned him in.

"Lamb, we've talked and it's been decided. You can join our fort, but!" I exclaimed and reached for the tall can and held it in front of him, "you must pass the can a teeth test."

"I'll do anything yous want, just tell me and I'll do it." He looked down at the wicked collection of dentures stacked tightly in the can, "Want me to take this some place?" A roar of laughs broke out and I held the can high above his billowed eyes.

"Reach in and take a couple out."

He dug deeply into the pile with an outstretched arm and removed a pair of perfect specimens caked with brown encrusted debris and yellow residue and examined them at arm's length from his body.

"Now try them out for size," I instructed. His head quivered in a hesitant shake and he looked about the room of doubting, cringing faces.

"Okay," and into his pink mouth they plunged. The dentures were larger than his teeth, both uppers and lowers, and he jiggled them about in his salivating mouth until they cradled snuggly around his teeth. His face swelled like a plump orange with the dentures protruding like a big car parked in a small garage, and his eyes looked more normal in size now that he had a bigger face. We drew back on our seats with a hushed reaction in frowns of disbelief. He did it. The other boys were founding members and didn't have to pass any test. Lamb and I were the only ones who ever had to taste the teeth.

    We slapped him on the back with delightful smacks, and his face shined in a bloated smile. He was now a proud member of the fort, but he would have to go through training. He placed a Roman helmet on his head without the protective Free Press. His head nestled into the tar bottom and the helmet hung over his large eyes. When he tried to take it off it stuck to his hair and he struggled removing it. In one swift move I yanked it from his head and he yelped in pain. "Never put one of these on without this," and I handed him a page of paper. We sat Lamb on a rusted bucket in the middle of the crowed shelter and began to school him on the ways of the fort.

Chapter 17
The Chump

The first day of July arrived and we were excited about the droves of summer residents that returned to Presque Isle County. There were 'Fudgies' and 'Lakies'; names we gave to those who invaded the county's state park campgrounds who invariably visited Mackinaw Island and the famous fudge shops, and families who came from 'down state' to open their musty lake cottages for a couple weeks of vacation. They wore sweatshirts with Michigan State plastered in big green letters and ones that displayed a large maize and blue M squarely in the center. They meandered through the town's shops and gathered around the Dairy Queen slurping on chocolate malts, or licking double sized ice cream cones in the warm summer evenings. They would, ultimately, assemble along Main Street in the thousands to watch the splendid 4th of July parade that was coming in a few days. Like sponges to spilled water, we sought out their conversations to learn cool new words and sayings so we could be the first to try them out and impress other kids in Chandlerville.

In the middle of the night a carnival procession crept into town in a long, secretive convoy beneath the humming streetlights along Main Street and parked in the field across from the funeral home. Every summer a carnival came to town before the 4th and fleeced the town with ill sighted gallery guns, under sized basketball hoops, and a haunted house where pick pocket artists operated in the dark. The carneys came in a wave of trucks pulling trailers of disassembled rides. There was the brightly colored tilt-a whirl hanging over a tandem flatbed, a skeletal frame of a Ferris wheel stacked in sections held down with clamped chains, short tag-a-long trailers pronouncing cotton candy, popcorn, and others were filled with stuffed teddy bears and gaudy trinkets all parked in rows making a midway.

The clang of sledgehammers pounding steel tent stakes woke us early and we dressed in a hurry to watch them erect the carnival. The night before Mom had given each of us a crisp ten-dollar bill for our carnival spending and I tucked mine securely in my back pocket. A crowd always gathered and got in the way of shady carnie workers with scruffy beards and grease soaked pants grumbling "ya can't stand there". I sat on the trampled grass near a shiny aluminum Airstream trailer that was parked near the cinderblock restrooms and watched a one-legged man stumble about trying to stretch a thick rope around a tent stake. My brothers wandered off through the collection of rides being assembled. The door opened on the Airstream and Petula Fricke stepped down to the grass and our eyes met in a warm gaze.

"Hi, I'm Toolie." My lips separated in hesitation and I was immediately caught off guard by her beauty. Like a stupefied moron I watched in awe and my mind raced in lofty visions of the two of us as she tossed her head back and flung her thick blond hair behind her slight shoulders. A gold-laced blue purse hung on a braided rope around her neck. Rosalie Smith, the dark haired sixth grader who participated in my first kiss was pretty with her bright green eyes. Donna Dorsey was cute when she wrapped her blonde hair in empty soup cans to make swirling curls that fell across her blue eyes when she winked at me, but the sight of Toolie Fricke's beauty knocked the voice out of me. All I could muster was 'huh' as I stared at her in admiration.

"What's a matter, cat got yer tongue?" She laughed.

Screaming in my head was the word 'decent' but I said, "Chris."

"You from... what's this town, Chandlerville?" She asked with her hands folded like angel wings in front of her blue dress.

"Yeah, I'm from here," I replied in a more comfortable voice, "you?"

Toolie swayed shifting her weight from hip to hip. She slowly spun herself around in a wistful circle like a ballerina doll in a music box with her hands holding the bottom of her dress, "Well, I guess I'm from all over. We never stay too long in one spot-always another show for us up the road, you know."

"Toolie," the peg-legged man working on the tent rope shouted, "you do those dishes, yet?"

"Yes sir, Dadda," she replied obediently in a slightly fearful response. The peg-legged carnie was her father, Jimbo Fricke. He had lost his leg while setting up the Ferris wheel for a show in Saugatuck ten years earlier. He was testing the freshly assembled ride when a large gear grabbed his pant leg and pulled him into the mashing gearbox and severed his left leg at the knee. He gave me a suspicious glance through his steel blue eyes and called Toolie over to the tent he was erecting. They spoke quietly and secretively so I couldn't hear. He pointed a stern greasy finger at her and she nodded and returned in a bouncing trot to where I was standing, "Wanna check out the set-up?"

I was willing to do anything with Toolie. We walked along the corridors of the rides and game stations and we talked about her life with the carnival. "Been to Detroit?" I asked.

"Lot's a times. Hate it," she remarked.

"Hey, maybe you know Tom Quarton? He's from Detroit," I asked as though she would know the boy I met last summer at Shoepac Lake.

She laughed, "There's a million people in Detroit. It's a big place, but maybe I met him once or twice, don't really recall, though," she said politely to my stupid question and did another twirl. "Let's go over to Gracie's and I'll introduce you to her."

We made our way past the cotton candy stand that was now opened for business and the roped off bowling pin game to a small travel trailer that was parked behind the carnival grounds. Toolie stepped close to the well-worn door and gave a soft rap with her fist.

"Be right there," a dainty and demure voice replied from behind the door.

"Yer gonna like Gracie," Toolie said and the door opened. In the low cut doorway appeared a woman still dressed in a green morning bathrobe and a towel wrapped around her dull red hair. She was tall and when she stooped forward to greet us her long tightly curled auburn beard glowed about her face in the morning sun. She was the carnival's bearded lady. I had never seen a bearded lady before. The closest I'd ever been to a woman with facial hair was Ruth Blake, the old woman with a hairy chin who lived on Twin Schools Road outside of town. Gracie stepped down from the trailer and confidently walked up to us.

"What do we have here? Bet you never saw a bearded lady before, have you?" She said, as she walked around me in a circle looking me up and down like a farmer bidding on a young bull at an auction. She placed her hand in front of me, and I took it in a hesitant shake. Her supple skin felt warm and certain in mine.

"Hi, my name's, Chris," I replied while trying not to look directly at her face.

"That's okay, Chris. Lots of people don't know how to look at me, but I'm used to it," she laughed; "one thing's for sure, you'll always remember me," and she laughed again.

Slowly, I became comfortable being with Gracie and her pleasant way and I told her my family owned the funeral home across the street. "Betcha yer 'old man' would be the last one to let a guy down," she joked. I had heard that one before. We had heard about every funeral home joke imaginable like, 'you stab 'em, we slab 'em', 'you eying me up for size?', and 'do you give discounts for walk in's?' She told us about the fun she had working as a side attraction and how she doubled as a monster in the House of Horrors.

Toolie and I left the bearded woman at her trailer, but before we departed Gracie called Toolie aside for a quick chat and then said she was glad to have met me. We walked along the busy midway that was now carrying out business with the gathering crowd. We stopped at the cotton candy trailer and I bought a couple of puffy pink treats. We held hands and smiled at each other with pink gooey faces and I told her about our stash of dynamite.

"What ya gonna do with that," she asked.

"Not sure yet, but it's gonna be fun," I boasted.

"Come over here," she said and pulled me toward a secluded area behind the row of parked diesel trucks. "I really dig you, Chris," she said in a sultry whisper. 'Dig'. I had never heard that word used in that context, and I was sure to add it to my vocabulary of cool sayings. She pulled me close to her blue dress and her body felt warm and firm as she pressed herself against me. She leaned her head closer to me and her blond hair smelled like summer. I felt her moist breath over my lips and we kissed. It wasn't a quick kiss like the one I stole from Rosalie Smith, it was a long and purposeful embrace and my body trembled wrapped in hers. She, gently, guided her hands along my back and across my hips and we remained locked together with her soft mouth absorbing mine. I fell in love with Toolie but our blissful embrace separated abruptly when we heard the clumsy peg-legged footsteps of Jimbo Fricke coming from behind the trucks. "We better go right now," she said anxiously and she tugged at my arm and pulled me back to the bustle of the midway crowd. "I've got to go now, but let's meet back here tonight, say, seven?" She turned in a quick glance, "It's been a real gas being with you."

I reached for her with my sweaty hands but she pulled away while blowing a kiss at me. "I can't wait," I said in love struck excitement. 'Gas'. There was another cool one for my lexicon.

Toolie darted off and I roamed the carnival grounds counting the minutes until our reunion at seven o'clock.

Verdie and Denis had disappeared in the maze of rides. Overhead were screams from thrilled kids strapped into the Blue Bullet as it rocked back and forth in a long semi-circle until it reached its apex and swung back down in a violent swoop. A never-ending organ played out an undistinguishable tune through black speaker boxes hoisted and clamped to metal poles across the midway. Lady Finger firecrackers strung together in grey powdery wicks crackled in snapping procession around the feet of mischievous young boys where they raced through the crowd.

Wide-eyed children perched on tiny saddles clung to plastic reins of brightly painted ponies that rose and fell like monotonous pistons as the carousel went round and round.

The smell of hot dogs cooking on rolling steel cylinders, popcorn bulging in striped paper bags, and swirling cotton candy collecting on paper handles collided in a pleasant mixture in the afternoon air. I walked among the crowd of carnival goers like a leaf that floats on a fall stream, getting lost within the mass of others drifting aimlessly in the current.

"Ay," a voice sounded from high above. It was Verdie and Willie leaning over the rail of a Ferris wheel gondola that was stalled as customers departed and new ones got on.

"Where the hell ya been?"

"Ah, just kickin' round down here," I replied in dull boredom.

"Seen Denis?"

"Nah, none of the usuals," I shouted, "I'll tell ya 'bout someone when yous come down."

"What?" Willie shouted and the giant wheel began to turn.

I knew they would be on the wheel for a while so I took a seat away from the midway and hoped for a familiar face to come by. It was near six o'clock and my appointment was coming soon. I could get a hot dog and smother it in onions and mustard and ketchup, but no, I didn't want onion breath when I kissed Toolie again. I decided on a frozen Coke and a bag of chips. The line of people standing in front of the snack vendor finally dissipated and a fat woman dressed in a ketchup-stained apron and dirty fingernails looked down at me, "What'll it be?" I gave her my order, "Fity cent," she said and plunked the items on the wet counter. I reached in my front pocket for the remaining four bits I had from the cotton candy change, and placed them in the puddle. I was thirsty and took a big draw from the straw and immediately went into a brain freeze. My head ached all the way back to my spot near the midway. People hurried about in all directions and bumped into each other like cattle in a staging pen while I sat waiting for Toolie, slowly enjoying my frozen Coke and chips.

It was after seven and I was getting desperate, Toolie hadn't arrived. Did I get the time wrong? Surely, something or someone had intercepted her, probably someone strapped in a peg leg, I reasoned.

I fidgeted in my eternal wait while the orange and red midway lights took over from the pale sunset. A pair of shadows walking hand and hand ducted behind the diesel trucks parked behind me. I could see one of the shadows wearing a blue dress spin gracefully in a slow turn like a ballerina in a music box, and nestle tightly to the other shadow in a long embrace. Lord, please don't let it be Toolie. I sneaked up near the shadows and crouched beside the wheel of a diesel. One shadow spoke to the other, "I really dig you, Everett," and the blue dressed shadow slowly ran her hands across the other's back and hips. A clumsy clop of a peg leg approached, "We've got to go right now, but let's meet in a couple hours." The shadows separated and one turned back to the other as they departed, "It's been a gas."

I leaned against a black tire and closed my eyes in heartbreaking darkness. I had been stripped of love like a thrasher through a wheat field leaving my thoughts in stubble. Composing myself, I decided to get that hot dog and smother it with as many onions it could hold.

The fat lady dropped the dog into a warm bun and jammed a red straw into a new frozen Coke, "fity cent."

I reached in my back pocket to grab a dollar, but the pocket was empty. I tried another pocket with the same results; empty. Then, like a rusty nail plunging through my tennis shoe, it hit me: a spinning ballerina in a blue dress had fleeced me.

"Fity cent, I said," barked the woman with dirty finger nails holding the hot dog, and then she concluded, "get outta here, ya chump."

I dragged my feet across the matted grass of the midway and took my familiar seat out of the way. I decided to keep quiet about my naïve behavior to save myself embarrassment. I couldn't stand the thought of the endless teasing I would endure from fort members. Behind me in the shadows, a peg-legged man held out his hand, a bearded lady and a blonde haired girl placed wads of cash into it and they parted hastily into the orange and red night. I thought of chasing after them but I didn't. In the midst of the busy midway a boy named Everett was turning his pockets inside out searching for something he had lost. I wasn't sure what Everett had learned that evening, but I learned a new word: chump.

Chapter 18
Boys and Bombs

    I turned on my side and held my pillow with both hands under my head. A puff of morning wind spilled through the bedroom window and I knew carnival dogs were cooking on their steel rollers across Main Street. My brothers were still sleeping and I heard Mom in the kitchen. She was making another surprise dinner dish and singing along to "Moon River" playing on the radio. Her voice blended beautifully with Andy Williams' as she harmonized perfectly in her smooth alto tone. The lyrics struck a familiar place in my mind when they came to, "you dream maker, you heart breaker," but felt relieved when it played, "I'm crossing you in style one day," and I smiled. The brothers began to wake and I sat up in bed.

    "Ahhh," Verdie stretched out beneath his sheet and Denis let out a similar wake-up grunt. "What a night. I think I rode every ride." On the side of Verdie's neck a circular purple blotch stuck out like an inkblot splattered on a sheet of white paper.

"Me, too," Denis yawned.

"What the hell's that?" I said examining the hickey from across the room, "Looks like that wasn't the only thing you was havin' fun with. Who was it?"

"Don't know what 'yer talkin' about," he replied in a puzzled yawn.

"You seen yer neck yet?"

"No."

Denis, now noticing the badge of achievement revealed, "Mary Reid. Saw you and her sneak behind the buses, and Willie was with her friend, Trudy."

Mary Reid, and her friend, Trudy Martin were a couple of eighteen-year old floozies who, at some point, had made out with most of the teenage boys in town. They lived in Tower and came to Chandlerville on the weekends to walk up and down Main Street looking for a good time, and sharing themselves with anyone with a car and full tank of gas. Last night it was Verdie and Willie's turn.

Verdie bounced from the bed and hurried to the dresser mirror. He stood in front of the mirror and turned from side to side inspecting the purple aftermath of his nocturnal encounter, "Man, she really got me. Decent."

"Better check the rest of 'yer body," I laughed and he started to pull his underwear down.

"What am I doin', she never got down there."

Denis jumped up and slugged him in the arm, "Hoke, joke, you owe me a coke," and we busted out laughing.

"Better not let Mom see that," I warned.

"Shit, man. I know," and he rubbed the blotch with his fingertips hoping it would disappear.

I went to the bathroom adjacent to our bedroom and took a large band aid from the medicine cabinet, "here, put this on."

"What did you do, last night?" Denis asked.

I knew this moment would come and I would have to tell them about my fun evening that never happened. I hadn't ridden a single ride and I was broke. I had a long time to think about it and made up a few scenarios I could follow, but they knew me well enough to know when I was lying. I wasn't going to tell them about Toolie, even if I had gotten a hickey.

"I learned a few cool words," and I sat on the edge of the bunk bed and dangled my feet above Denis' bunk.

"Oh yeah, let's hear 'em," Verdie asked.

"Well, there's 'dig' and 'gas'."

"Dig and gas, 'ay? What's cool about 'em?"

"It's how you use 'em. Like, 'I really dig yer car, it's a real gas'."

"I see," Verdie, thought for a moment," they are cool," and said, "I dig it."

"Gas. That's funny. I got some gas," Denis chuckled.

"Nah, you don't use it like that," I said.

"I know, I'm just shittin' 'ya," and we laughed. I didn't tell them about the other word I learned.

The sounds of a piano plinking out inharmonious tones stopped when Carol Post finished giving her lesson. Craig poked his head through an open window and called to us across the narrow space between Flynn's and the funeral home. "We meetin' this mornin'?"

"Yeah, see you there at nine," Verdie shouted.

There was a meeting scheduled at the fort that I didn't know about and we dressed quickly to make it there by nine am. We hurried through the kitchen and grabbed a buttered toast from a stack sitting on the table. Verdie hoped Mom wouldn't notice the large Band-Aid on his neck, but she did. "What's that?"

"Ran into a branch," I quickly replied and we rushed down the back stairs and headed for the fort.

There was a lot to go over. We hadn't convened since the carnies arrived and we were anxious to hear what each had done at the carnival. One by one, the members arrived and the carnival organ played in the distance and people began to gather at the rides and mill around the midway. Each of us had their chance to tell their story but I listened pensively in silence. I was completely implacable with the idea that I had been duped; taken advantage of, made into a chump. There had to be a way of getting even with the carnies and I would wait for an opportunity but needed help. I couldn't ask any of the fort guys; that would mean I would have to hold a chump's confession. My mind began to steam like a teapot.

After the stories were told in their distorted and embellished recollections, Willie and Verdie changed the topic to dynamite. After all, we were in possession of the best firecrackers one could have, and they were determined to put them in use, but how and where? The chemistry boys had a plan. "We know how to set off the dynamite," Willie declared. We listened intently as he explained; "Yous guys know how we make those blue tip firecrackers in aluminum foil?"

"Yeah."

"That's gonna' be our detonation cap."

"Shit, man, think that'll do it?" Craig said.

"Hell yeah, but we need to set off the match heads with another smaller explosion-a Lady Finger," Verdie explained

"That's it! That'll make a bigger boom and wolla, the big ka-boom!" Willie said with his arms held apart like they were exploding; "But where? We have another plan."

"The night of the 4th is when they ar' gonna have the fireworks, right?" We nodded. "With all of the explosions going off who's gonna' notice ours, should fit right in;" Verdie finished the plot.

Every 4th of July, Chandlerville put on a fireworks display. The town's merchants placed plastic jugs by their countertop tills for donations. The meager contributions weren't enough to buy all of the fireworks needed to put on a decent show. So, each year, Lou Maxon, the rich advertising agency owner from Detroit, who grew up in Chandlerville, donated the remaining money needed for the holiday display. Maxon had, also, donated the block of land behind Hartman's Standard Gas station where the city built baseball diamonds and it was appropriately named, 'Maxon Field'. On the south end of town, two high, sloping hills converged by the high school. The town's water tower stood in peeled paint at the top of the highest hill we called the Lockies. The adjoining hill was called the Loops. A view of the entire town could be seen from there. The

Chandlerville Fire Department used the Loops for setting off the fireworks. The holiday was a day away and we would be ready. We parted company and headed for the carnival.

The midway crowd looked the same as it did the night before as patrons carried babies, and older kids ran from one attraction to another. The smell of carnival cooking was the same, too, and I sat at my station in a doleful gaze while everyone else was having fun. Through the gathering people I saw Everett Duncan making his way in a slow shuffle looking as forlornly as I. As he approached a thought came to mind and hit me like a splash of cold water; I bet he wants revenge, too. I had seen Duncan a few times before when he first moved to town in May. He was my age and would, probably, be in my grade when school started. I watched him mope through the crowd dressed in blue jean cut-offs that showed ragged and frayed edges, a brown and yellow striped shirt and red tipped high-top white socks covering his feet inside brown leather sandals. He looked like a dork. Much like the night before, his eyes combed the discarded candy wrappers and empty popcorn bags that lay strewn on the midway ground as though he was still searching for something. He was close enough now where I didn't have to yell to get his attention, "Ay." Everett looked around to see where my voice came from. Another 'ay' and he looked my way. "Loose somethin'?" I asked.

Everett walked closer, and politely responded, "I'm not sure, but I might have lost some money here last night."

"Chris," I nodded.

"Everett," he nodded.

I tried to be tactful with my approach so I wouldn't offend him but decided to just lay it out as I saw it. "You met someone here last night, didn't you?" He gave me a puzzled look.

"Yeah, I met two people."

"One named Toolie and the bearded lady, Gracie?" I asked. "Did ya see a peg-legged guy the girl call Dadda, too?"

"Yeah, how'd you know that?"

"I met the same people yesterday and I seen you with Toolie behind the diesels," I said and he tried not to believe it. I told him about my encounter with the carnie crew and our stories were nearly identical. We reasoned they worked as a pickpocket team in every town they went to. Toolie with her ballerina dance and wandering hands, Gracie sizing up the victim and letting Toolie know what pocket held the cash and doubling as a monster in the House of Horrors so she could pick the pockets of the naive thrill seekers, and Jimbo Fricke acting as the drop off guy.

"What can we do now; they got twenty bucks from me. How much did they get from you?" He asked.

"Bout ten," I said. "They're probly' out there right now doin' the same thing, ya know." I paused then asked, "Wanna' get even?"

"Hell, yeah. But how we do that?"

"Whatdaya say we just kinda stroll around and see if we can find 'em. We can't be together, though. They'd figure it out right away if they saw us."

So, we set out on a search and destroy mission. I took one side of the carnival and he searched the other. We peered into concession stands, we looked at every ride, I, even, went behind the House of Horrors trailer and tried to open a door but it was locked. Finally, there was Toolie with another victim, holding hands and walking through the far end of the midway out to a row of parked cars. I motioned to Everett and he saw her, too. I held my hand up and motioned for him duck low so he wouldn't be seen and we sneaked behind a stack of storage crates to observe the pair. It was the same routine as ours; the embrace, the roaming hands, the peg-legged interruption, and a boy left with empty pockets.

"Let's follow Jimbo, he's got the money. Let's see what he does with it." I suggested and Everett agreed.

Through the parked cars and behind the diesels and away from the crowd, Jimbo hobbled away on his peg leg carrying the gold laced, blue purse that Toolie had around her neck. Toolie returned to the midway. We stalked the stumpy carnie like a pair of coyotes' following a wounded deer until he reached the shiny aluminum Airstream trailer where he slid a key into the locked door and went inside.

"What now?" Everett asked in a hushed tone.

"We need some kinda distraction ta get him outta the trailer," I whispered and we plotted our next move hiding next to the cinder block bathrooms out of his view. "You got any firecrackers?"

"Yeah, a got a cherry bomb I was saving for the 4th," he said.

"Shit, man. Perfect. Decent. Here's the plan…" and Everett ran off to get his cherry bomb.

I waited and watched the Airstream diligently like a sniper in a ground blind and hoped Jimbo Fricke didn't leave the trailer. Everett returned with the red ball bomb and sneaked up to where I was, trying to conceal his heavy breathing from his four-block sprint. A cherry bomb was the closest thing to dynamite we could lay our hands on. It was round and red and about the size of a magnum marble with a stubby short wick. I knew I had about five seconds, or less, to light it and find a hiding place. If my plan worked, I would have a chance to get in the trailer and reclaim our money.

"Ready?" I whispered. Everett took a deep breath and handed me the bomb and a book of matches. I sneaked up to the trailer on my tiptoes like a cagy cat and held the wick to a lit match and placed the red ball on the metal step in front of the trailer door. Everett took his place about ten yards away from the trailer and waited for the explosion. I sprinted off to hide behind the bathrooms. 'Kaboom' went the cherry bomb and the concussion sprung the door open. A dazed Fricke stumbled to the doorway and waved at the blue smoke trying to figure out what had happened. There stood Everett, proudly displaying an erect 'bird' finger to the confused Fricke. Collecting himself, the now alert carnie screamed,

"You little sumbitch!" and took chase in hopping leaps after the swift 'bird' boy. There was no chance of him catching Everett, but he tried. A hop, and a skip, a hop, and a skip went the sweaty, tee shirted mono-legged culprit in vain pursuit. Here was my chance. I sprinted to the trailer and rushed inside. The entrance led directly to the kitchen where recently washed dishes were neatly stacked on a towel across a pink counter top. My eyes quickly combed the confines and I saw the gilded blue purse setting on the kitchen table. Sitting next to the purse was a partial roll of carnival ride tickets. I spread the purse open and a crumbled wad of bills spilled out. There were ten's, twenties and a gob of ones mixed in between. Back out the door I ran through the settling smoke while the muffled shouts of a peg-legged man blended in with the carnival noise as he chased the fleet footed 'bird' boy to no avail.

Everett and I met behind the Dairy Queen and hour later, and greeted each other with broad smiles and slaps to the back celebrating our retribution.

"You were perfect, Chris." Everett laughed.

"So were you," I said returning the compliment. "Did you see the look on his face when he came to the door? Man, yer fast," I said.

We had pulled it off; everything went according to our brave plan. I hadn't counted the money yet so we found a private seat on the lawn behind the Dairy Queen, and spread the cash out in front of us. There was sixty-seven dollars. Everett's face lit up when I pulled the partial roll of ducats from inside my shirt, "Whaddaya think about this?" I said, tossing the roll on the grass.

"What a gas!" he said, and we rolled on our backs laughing hysterically.

We returned to the carnival that evening. The orange red glow of the midway lights pierced through the dull haze of cigarette, cigar and firecracker smoke. It was the busiest night of the three-day carnival. A character dressed in Uncle Sam attire walked carefully about the crowd on tall stilts wearing a red, white and blue striped top hat and pants barking, "Get yer tickets, get yer tickets here," but Everett and I didn't need any. We bolted from ride to ride trying to take them all on in one night.

We handed them out freely to everyone we knew. We gave a long strip to the Cassidy kids, another dozen to the three Clementson brothers, and pretty soon we had a line of beggars following us as though we were a pair of ticket pied pipers.

Everett and I split company and I went looking for the fort members so I could share my tickets with them. The tickets could be used for any ride and anything at the concession stands; they were good for any purchase.

The carnival was in high gear now with every ride jammed with people and long lines waiting to get on. Verdie, Denis and Froggy were waiting for a seat on the Tilt A Whirl. I ran up and passed them a couple dozen ducats. Craig, Johnny and Willie were gathered nearby at the concession stand waiting to buy hot dogs. I tore a long strip from the remaining roll and handed them over.

"Where the hell did ya get these?" They said astonished and grateful. I had about as much carnival fun as I could stand for the day and headed home.

Chapter 19
The Rescue and the Parade

    I dragged myself to my bedroom and took a seat on my top bunk, exhausted from the carnival activity. There was still a lot of carnival left, but I thought 'better not hang around the midway' for fear of being found by the carnie crooks. I could hear Pa speaking French on the phone and Mom sat at the kitchen table and listened. I knew he must have been speaking with one of my Uncles, and I could understand some of what he was saying but not enough to know everything. It was his younger brother, Jacques, on the phone. "Bien, je sais," he said to Jacques. "Mais je ne peux pas vous donner l'argent. Je suis desole." I knew he was declining a request for money.

    My father was raised in a French speaking settlement in North Dakota. The village had paid for part of Grandpa's medical schooling at Laval University in Montreal, Canada, if he would spend a certain amount of time repaying the loan by practicing medicine in their town. After his indentured service, Napoleon and Emma

Cosette moved Pa and his three brothers to Port Austin, Michigan. Pa was eight years old and out of place knowing only French in an English-speaking town; all of the brothers only spoke French. Jacques was the youngest child. When he was a teenager growing up in the Lake Huron port town, he and his best friend, Arnie Parks had built a sailboat. On its maiden voyage the mast broke and the boat capsized in the violent waves. Arnie Parks drowned but Jacques survived; he claimed the Virgin Mary carried him back to the overturned boat where he was later found and rescued. He never got over the death of his friend and blamed himself for the accident because he was manning the rudder. This wasn't the only time he had a vision. He and a group of friends hunted deer in the Upper Peninsula every fall. They always did well but one year Jacques became lost in the wilderness near Newberry. He was lost for two days and said he was saved when the Virgin Mary appeared to him again and led him to safety. Mom felt he was blessed. To have seen the Blessed Mother, not once, but twice was a miracle in her mind. He became withdrawn and acted strangely in the years to follow; failing at every business venture he tried. This time it was a 'speculation' home he was building in Bad Axe, and like all his other ill planned money making endeavors, he was out of cash. Pa had bailed him out before, but not this time. Jacques was on his own and was going to lose the house to the bank.

    Pa placed the yellow phone back on its hook, "He wants money, but I'm not going to give it to him. He still owes us tree-taowsand from the last big deals. He's pretty upset an' was cryin'." Mom said nothing but would have been supportive if the money was given. It was Pa's call. I lay on my bed in the warm evening and a shallow breeze struggled to invade the room, but my cotton sheets felt cool to my skin. I waited for Verdie and Denis to return, and thought nothing more of the phone conversation.

    As usual, I was the first to awake while my brothers slept twisted in their sheets like worn out carnival soldiers. They had slipped into the bedroom without my knowing during the night. I could smell coffee perking on the woodstove. The 4th of July had finally arrived and I couldn't believe they could sleep knowing what the day was going to hold for us. First thing was to meet at the fort.

We hadn't seen Lamb at the carnival, but he showed up at the fort that Wednesday morning. His father was off the boat for a few days and took him and his mom to Mackinaw Island for a few days. He was glad to be back with us. "Whad I miss," he said wearing his new fudgy Mackinaw Island sweatshirt. We never told him about the dynamite until now and filled him in on the plan. I'm not sure if he fully understood what dynamite could do. The only time he ever saw anything done with it was on The Roadrunner cartoons where Wile E. Coyote is forever getting blown up with Acme Dynamite. Hell, none of us really knew what to expect. All of the members were gathered in the fort and it was crowded. We rehearsed the plan and everyone knew to meet at the Loops before dark.

"This is what's gonna do it, boys," and Willie displayed a small sheet of aluminum foil and a box of Ohio Blue Tip matches. Verdie produced a string of Lady Finger firecrackers and unraveled one. We peered over their shoulders while they began assembling the miniature bomb. Like a demolition team, they snapped the heads from the matchsticks and placed a half-dozen tips on the piece of foil. They folded the edges of foil together and twisted the top closed. Verdie took a Lady Finger and pushed it through the foil then dripped some candle wax over the edge of the firecracker to seal them together.

"Okay, this is it," Verdie said and held up the contraption for all of us to view. "Let's try it," and we stepped outside and Willie lit it. The small device went off with a respectable bang and blew a small indentation into the clay.

"That should be just enough," Willie reasoned and we were impressed. So it was off to Main Street and the gathering people.

Chandlerville put on a grand parade every year and the procession was going to start at twelve-noon. Main Street would fill up before that with Lakies and Fudgies jamming the sidewalks and stores. The mass of people sauntered along Main Street licking popsicles, and draining malted shakes through plastic straws like cattle grazing in a pasture of people. I didn't recognize any of the downstate invaders. Lamb and I shuffled slowly behind the wave of people. Ahead of us, I noticed a staggering Booz Danker. He held his burning cigarette chest high in his bronze hand and smiled at the hoard of people passing him by as though he was a one-man welcoming team for Chandlerville. The crowd moved in stuttered steps, and would pause for a moment and resume its snail's pace. A man in a brown rayon shirt walking in front of Booz stopped and Booz's cigarette touched the man's sleeve leaving a small black mark that began to smolder. Soon the black patch spread like a grass fire, and the man brushed at the small inferno as though a hive of bees were stinging him. When the man discovered he was on fire he ripped the burning shirt from his chest and stomped on it to extinguish the smoking flames. Booz, not knowing he set the man afire continued ahead and bumped into the next person igniting her cotton purse in the same fashion as the man with the rayon shirt. Suddenly, two people were putting fires out. Finally, Booz dropped the cigarette and staggered over to a bench and took a seat smiling innocently at the passersby, never realizing what he had accomplished. Lamb and I laughed and continued up the street while the two fire victims swatted and stomped frantically amidst the crowd.

Lamb stopped suddenly and yelped, and then I felt a burning sting on my temple, then another. Lamb yelped in agony, again. Small welts began to rise on his neck and on my cheek and temple. We cringed in pain. Hiding amidst the cover of the crowd stood Bill Pratt holding his peashooter at his chest trying to look inconspicuous, but giggling at the profound accuracy of his well-placed shots. Fred Millender stood beside Pratt and snickered our way with glaring eyes. Lamb rubbed at the welts and I pulled him out of the way and we sprinted through the crowd. Pratt and Millender followed in pursuit spraying green peas at us like bursts of lead from a machine gun. The pellets pinged off the lampposts and on our bodies as we ran. I saw Chubba Harkins, and Farny McIntosh leaning on the fender of Chubba's rust-colored '49 Plymouth parked in front of the Post Office. Chubba stopped us when he saw what was going on. "Hey, what the hell ya think yoah doin'?" he shouted at Pratt and Millender. He and Farny saw the welts on our bodies and stepped toward the pair. I was caught off guard when Chubba came to our defense. He seemed never to care about his younger brother, Johnny, much less Lamb and me.

"Ra...ra...real ha...ha...hard asses ain't ya's?" Farny stuttered while puffing up his chest in contempt.

"Try that shit on us 'Puahcy' and you'll see what happens to ya's," Chubba challenged and lit the 'Percy' fuse to Pratt's abominable temper. "Didn't ya learn anything last week when Cliffahd put ya down?" Reminding him of the brief exchange they had when Clifford Krupp repeatedly called him 'Perce Evil' and humiliated Pratt earlier in the day he died at the Ruins.

Pratt's nostrils flared and he clenched his fists in anger but he knew enough to step back from an encounter with Chubba and Farny. The Frenchtown pair retreated and in a poisonous response, Pratt yelled as he was running away, "Yeah, where's yer buddy now, Harkins? Deader than a doornail! Cried like a baby all the way down, didn't he?"

Chubba stood quietly next to Farny, and his head hung to his chest with the sad reminder. He was perplexed with Pratt's words; how would he know anything about Clifford's fall? He and Farny slid past the Plymouth's doors and Chubba turned the key. The souped up V-8 flathead, that he and Clifford rebuilt to perfection, rumbled out a husky gurgle through its glass-pack mufflers, and

Chubba leaned out the window, "Keep as fah away from those assholes as ya can."

I stepped to the driver's door, "Thanks, man," and they peeled down First Street. We headed back up town to seek the safety of our group, watching the crowd carefully for any sign of the Frenchtown gang.

High up on the street lights, American flags flapped in the occasional breeze. Bernie Snyder peddled by on a tricycle, with a cooler filled with ice and pop attached to the handlebars, selling soft drinks to thirsty parade folks. The man from the carnival dressed in Uncle Sam clothes, towered over us on his stilts, stepping carefully through the crowd. Main Street was packed with people waiting for the parade to start.

We made it to the Metropole Bar. People poured in and emptied out in a constant flow. Roger Madden, who was known as 'Rah', stood on the bandstand and plunked at his acoustic six-string, singing 'Walk On By'. The song spilled out from the speakers hanging above the front door and some folks heeded the lyrics and some didn't. A loud shrill from Lloyd Levin's police car siren screamed above the crowd noise and the parade began. A County Sheriff's Deputy walked ahead of the oncoming floats to move the crowd to the sidewalks. A cacophonous clatter of air horns, whistles, marching band drums and brass instruments fell on the crowd like a giant tidal wave. Hands full of candy were flung to eagerly awaiting kids rushing to the adorned edges of the different floats. Cameras clicked wildly when Miss Chandlerville, and her court majestically rolled by with their porcelain smiles and cupped hands waiving to the crowd in monotonous repetition. We took our place at the edge of the parade and forgot about the welts on our faces.

A two-o'clock sun blistered above the scorched crowd, and the parade floats dispersed through the side streets. A Chandlerville Fire truck straddled Main Street opposite a polished Millersburg fire truck parked twenty yards away. Between them sat an aluminum beer barrel in the street. Every year the neighboring towns' fire departments held a contest to see who could force the barrel to the other team's side with their water hoses. The teams of firefighters faced off like gunfighters waiting to draw as a sweaty crowd gathered around. Waves of water sprayed on the sweltering people from errant aiming and a rainbow appeared in the mist. We fort members stood together in a humble flock letting the bursts of water cascade over us in a cool drenching. Chandlerville won the beer barrel contest. There were long hours to wait before darkness would arrive and the anticipated fireworks display. Like church letting out, we dispersed from Main Street to our homes, and waited for the evening to come.

Chapter 20
The Grand Finale

Eight-thirty, July 4th. The town had settled down at the culmination of the three-day festival. Main Street looked bare. Toolie, and the other carnies were leaving in the morning and had begun their carnival breakdown. But Fudgies and Lakies would assemble one more time in parked cars along the roads leading to Chandlerville to watch the coup de gras of the holiday; the fireworks. The sun was setting behind a mass of rain clouds as we assembled at the fort. We hoped it wouldn't rain. That would delay the fireworks until the next day. Lamb was the only one missing. Verdie and Willie had made several of the foil blasting caps and kept them securely in their jean pockets. We stood outside the fort, nervously hashing out the details of the coming episode. Behind the burlap door, in a canvas bag, sat a whole stick of dynamite, now covered in a white powder.

"We better not go up there in a group, someone's gonna' wonder what's goin' on," Verdie said.

"Verdie and I, and Chris and Denis will go in one group. Johnny, Froggy, and Craig, yous guys come behind us." Willie said, "And let us know if yer' bein' followed."

We set out for the Loops in a catlike stealth to build a launch pad. Willie carried the canvas bag cradled in his arms like it was a newborn baby. We hiked closely behind him along College Street, past Edna's Party Store and the school, and onto the sloping, grassy hill of the Loops. We sneaked on tiptoes so the fire department wouldn't hear us while they assembled their launch pad. A half-dozen men in canvas bib overalls stretched long wire cables to the launch pad from a wooden control box. Their flashlights beamed like bright fireflies over the ground where they worked. Beside the launch area sat a fire truck with its running lights on, and its hose laying on the grass, poised for a possible emergency.

We crawled on our bellies atop the stiff weeds and sand with the determination of snipers getting into position for a shot. We were within a hundred yards from the fireworks launch area at a place we thought was perfect. We were on the down slope of the Loops, on a small rise, and far enough away from the fireworks crew to stay unnoticed. Johnny, Craig and Froggy took a safe spot adjacent to us on the side of the Lockies several hundred yards away.

The first salvo of a giant bottle rocket shot out of its tube and made a 'thump' sound when it hurled itself into the dark sky leaving a bright trail of orange sparks, then, 'boom'. The sky lit up in a spectacular flare of red, white and blue fiery sprinkles drifting down in tiny parachutes illuminating the ground where we lay. We hugged the grass as tightly as we could for fear of being seen, but then it was dark again. The blaring of car horns sounded their approval in the distance and several more rockets were launched in secession. Booms, and blasts, and honking car horns echoed across the Chandlerville night like a bombing raid underway. It was time for our contribution to the festival.

Willie hollowed out a hole in the sand with his sweaty hands and placed the dynamite stick inside. Verdie had fashioned a long wick on the Lady Finger that would give him time to escape the explosion. "Take off yous guys," Willie cried through the booming and banging overhead. We sprinted away as fast as we could and dove to the ground waiting for Willie and the blast. We could see the faint flare of a match ignite and wick sparkle. Willie's footsteps raced toward us in the dark and he let out a groan when he dove to his chest with a thud next to us. Suddenly, the earth shook and erupted with a discharge unlike anything we had ever heard before. Grey sand and stone rose from the ground in a volcanic spew of blinding flames and flash. The concussion force struck us head on like tidal wave and rolled us over on our backs. The firefighters standing near the launch pad were knocked to the ground in a daze and the fire truck rocked on its wheels. Then all hell came forth as the remainder of the fireworks began to explode where they lay stacked between us and the launch pad.

Fireworks with delicate flower names like Peony, Dahlia and Chrysanthemum bulleted ferociously across the crest of the Loops setting the dry grass on fire. Poppers, spinners, strobes and snakes careened off the white ball of the water tower and spun aimlessly across the sky in a fizz of sparks. The entire area was besieged with multi-colored fireworks exploding at ground level with some shooting skyward. Small pebbles and sand began to descend on us and a putrid smell of sulfur hung in the air. By now, the firemen were shooting blasts of water at the flames racing through the grass. Another fire truck was dispatched to help put out the fires, and it groaned its way up College Street with its lights flashing, and siren screaming. A deep crater had formed where the dynamite went off and smoldered harmlessly when the night sky opened up in a heavy downpour. The fireworks were over.

By the time we reached the coal bin door, Verdie was already in the basement. Denis and I crawled across the black chunks of coal taking deep breaths trying to catch our wind from the long race back to the safety of our home. A dim light hung from the rafters above the stone basement walls and we brushed at the black dust that soaked into our wet pants. Verdie was sitting with his elbows on the wooden work counter holding his drenched head in hands, "Shit man, are we in trouble."

A dour countenance marked our faces where we stood in the narrow room, much like the acrid smell of gunpowder and sulfur had soured the air on top of the Loops. The blast had left us in shock and we hadn't fully recovered in its aftermath. In our retreat, we managed to skirt the police cars that raced to the firework's scene and we saw Pa speeding up College Street in the blue hearse. Was he summonsed as an ambulance or for a 'call'? An explosion of remorseful guilt erupted inside us while we wondered if we had caused injuries, or maybe a death?

The rain falling on the metal coal bin door sung out loudly. We heard the Ford hearse stop beside it in the alley. The driver's door slammed and we waited expectantly to hear the rear doors open but they didn't. There was a great sigh of relief among us; there must not have been an injury or death, Pa was back home far too soon for either. Above the basement walls where we hid, Pa's steps ascended the steep stairs to the apartment.

"How are we ever going to get away with this?" Denis asked.

"Guys, who else knows what we were gonna do? I didn't tell anyone, did yous guys?" Verdie said defensively.

"Come on, we been talkin' at the fort all the time. Maybe Johnny or Craig, or Froggy spilled the beans." I reasoned, "Nah, they know better," then I remembered what I said to Toolie, "Oh, oh."

"What?" Verdie asked.

"I may have screwed up," I fessed up and told them the story about meeting Toolie, Gracie and Jimbo Fricke. They sat close to me on their wobbly stools, and listened intently as I went into the specific details. They bristled when I spoke of how Toolie played me and Everett for chumps, and how she, Gracie and the 'peg leg' worked as a team.

"Why didn't you tell us?" Denis demanded, "we could a done somethun'."

"I was too embarrassed," I said, and when I explained how Everett and I got revenge they perked up in pride.

"Wayda' go, Chris. I was wonderin' how you got all those tickets," Verdie said.

"I still got twenty bucks left from the purse, too," I revealed.

"We don't know if they even suspect us," Verdie concluded. "Let's just play dumb and wait and see what happens next."

It was time now to make our way upstairs. It was late and it was raining harder. "I don't think we should go in all together." I said.

"Yer right. You and Denis take the back stairs and I'll wait a while and then come up."

Our next challenge was getting to our bedroom unnoticed, but there was no chance of that. Pa had just hung up the phone. Mom was clutching her rosary and praying where she was sitting on the green couch in the living room.

"Where's Verdie," Pa asked, and sat down next to Mom.

"Isn't he home?" I replied.

"No."

Just then Verdie entered the room and we stood in front of them, dripping wet and besieged with a barrage of questions.

"Where yous been, tonight?"

"Up town, just hangin' round," Verdie answered.

"Were yous up at da fireworks?" Came the next question.

"Ah, sorta," I hesitated.

"Den yous know what happened."

"No... I don't thinks so... I thought they were a little weird...not much to 'um," Denis hesitated.

"You didn't notice dat someting' was different? An dat most a da fireworks went off on da ground?" Pa said and leaned toward us and placed his Frankenmuth on the table. "Don't suppose yous know anyting about dat, ay?"

"Was that what happened?" Verdie meekly responded.

"I got called to da Loops by Lloyd Levin, and he said bring da ambulance. When I got dare it look like a war zone. Da entire hill had caught on fire when da fireworks exploded on da ground. Doz' firemen said someone set off dynamite and damn near killed dem all."

"Anybody get hurt?" I asked while I recited an Our Father in the back of my mind.

"No, but dare wasn't one eyebrow or mustache left on any a dare faces."

We kept any sign of relief hidden from our faces, but were thankful. At the very least, a hand or an eye might have been blown away, or worse.

"Get those wet clothes off now and get to yer room," Mom said and pointed a firm finger toward our bedroom.

We stacked our wet clothes outside the bedroom door and sprawled out on our beds. The room remained quiet as we lay on our backs and stared at the ceiling thinking about the havoc we had created on the Loops. Was it a dream we had witnessed, or a nightmare? It was us who had ruined the evening for all of the Lakies and Fudgies, and Chandlerville kids. I wondered if Willie and the rest of the fort's members were grilled when they got home like us. Did any of them spill the beans in forced confessions? No, I thought, we were too tough for parental interrogation. We could hack it; we were brave members of our beloved fort. Then, I realized what Father Klein meant when he screamed at us; we truly were the Dregs of Presque Isle.

"Think it's over, guys?" Denis said in sleepy voice.

"Not in a coon's age," Verdie replied.

Across Main Street, a steady drizzle of rain fell upon the carnies as they banged sledgehammers against steel tent stakes, and wrapped long ropes in twinned coils throughout the night and into the morning.

The sound of diesel trucks firing up in a low rumbling clatter woke me. The bedroom was still with my brothers sleeping in the dim morning light. I stretched and yawned, and rolled to my side. I listened as the carnies put their final cinches on the tie-down chains. I thought about Toolie, and her hands on my skin; her spinning ballerina twirls. I remember how she blew a flirtatious kiss at me as she walked away with my money in her gold edged purse.

She was going to be leaving soon, and I would never see her again. I wondered if she would remember me, or was I going to be a faceless mark like all the others she had swindled. I dressed quickly and rushed down the long stairway and through the door onto Main Street. I wanted a final revengeful peek. The diesels were lining up like horses at a starting gate with the carcasses of rides disassembled and strapped on their flatbed trailers. At the head of the procession was a yellow Ford pickup hitched to a shiny aluminum Airstream trailer. Jimbo Fricke was behind the wheel and a sleepy blond leaned against the passenger door. When the yellow Ford pulled on to Main Street, Toolie laid her face on her folded arms across rolled down window opening and looked my way. I stood on the side of the curb with the blue purse dangling in my hand. Her face held a look of satisfaction as her eyes glared at me. I began swinging the purse in a circle and glared back. Her angry eyes followed me as the truck pulled away. I spun myself in a slow swirl like a ballerina in a music box, and blew a kiss at her as she drove away.

Chapter 21
The Blue Statues

    Eggs sizzled in a cast iron skillet and bacon crackled in another as Mom made breakfast. We sat at the breakfast table quietly trying not to give any reason for her to resume the conversation from the night before. We could see she was still leery of our version of the fireworks fiasco and the possibility that we were somehow involved. She knew us well and what we were capable of. She slid a couple of 'over easys' on my plate, and I dipped the tip of a brown slice of toast into their yellow pools. Denis took a couple of slices of bacon from the plate sitting in the middle of the table and crumbled them onto his eggs. Verdie sat next to me, and drew on a sketchpad and ignored the eggs on his plate. He dragged the pencil in skillful waves and swirls over the paper. I watched as an image started to appear. The grey swirls transformed into billowing smoke, and the stringy lines became trails of fireworks jetting from the ground and into the sky. Appearing through the smoky haze collected on the ground he drew four crouching figures in the foreground with eyes bulging wide open. They looked remarkably like Willie, and us. I gave Verdie a stiff elbow to his side, and I had trouble keeping the giggle inside me. Denis turned his forehead into a frown and moved his lips in a silent 'stop it' gesture while trying to contain his laughter.

The sound of a firm knock on the apartment door broke our attention to the drawing. Pa rose from the couch, and opened the door. Two Michigan State Police troopers, standing erect like two purposeful statues, dressed in blue with shiny badges, were in the doorway. Their black-billed hats sat snuggly on their heads and their uniforms were impeccably neat like they had been painted on. The patent leather shoes they wore glistened like shiny black mirrors. They entered the room, and a brief conversation took place at the entranceway. Our names were called out in Pa's harsh voice, and we marched slowly in a guilty gait over to the interrogators. A tall, handsome trooper who looked remarkably like Elvis, held a note pad and spoke, "I'm Trooper Terry Riley, and this is Trooper Phillip Moore," he said nodding to the broad shouldered statue standing beside him. "How are you boys this morning?"

We rolled back and forth on our heels and fidgeted nervously with culpable faces. "Okay," I replied.

"We're here because of what happened last night." said Trooper Phillip Moore; "and, I believe you boys know what I'm talking about. We have Willie Hanson out in our cruiser right now so you boys should tell us the truth."

We brothers looked at each other with helpless glances. I could feel the beads of sweat forming on my forehead, and my stomach began to ache. My head spun in a dizzying array of excuses and fabrications of the truth that were, before now, never hard to conjure up. I couldn't think of anything to deflect the truth, and they had Willie locked in their cruiser like a dangerous criminal.

The sound of someone climbing the steps to our apartment broke the momentary silence, and Lloyd Levin entered the room. Pa stepped over to him and they held a brief hushed conversation. The staunch troopers stood before us and waited for our reply.

"We didn't think anything like this was ever gonna happen," Verdie admitted holding his head low in guilt. "We was just tryin' ta have some fun but it got outta hand."

"You are aware that someone could have been injured badly or even killed last night," Trooper Riley said adding more guilt. "Did you boys see the hole left in the ground?"

We nodded.

"Now, do you have any more dynamite?"

I looked at Verdie, Verdie looked at Denis, Denis looked at Verdie. "Yeah, we got a few more sticks," the reluctant Verdie confessed.

"Where?" The trooper asked.

A gloom spread across Verdie's face like someone had taken a grimy hand and smeared it on. Denis and I never knew where he put the dynamite. We couldn't have answered the question if we wanted to. I felt relieved in a fleeting moment of innocence. Verdie looked toward our parent's bedroom just a few steps from where we stood. "Over there," he said while pointing with his eyes.

Pa's eyes widened, "Sacre!" Mom clutched her hands together. The two troopers stepped back and looked at each other suspiciously, "Are you saying the dynamite is in the house?" Trooper Riley uttered.

"Yeah, it's under their bed," Verdie admitted.

A frantic scene got underway, and the troopers took us abruptly by our limp arms, "Everyone out of the house right now," Riley demanded. Pa took Mom by the hand and rushed to the door. Lloyd Levin led the way down the steep stairs and onto the sidewalk. A brand new Plymouth Fury State Police cruiser sat at the curb with a dejected Willie slumped in the back seat. Trooper Moore jumped onto the front seat and grabbed the microphone from the dash and spoke, "This is Trooper Moore dispatched to four-two-nine Main Street, Chandlerville calling Gaylord post. We need assistance with dynamite removal from a residence, over."

A crackling voice replied, "Sending special unit to your site; will arrive within an hour. Over."

Trooper Riley opened the back door of the cruiser. "Get in," and we took a seat next to Willie.

We said nothing to each other as we sat in remorse across the plastic seat of the cruiser. Willie's face was long and worried. His unbuttoned shirt, unlaced shoes and crusty eyes revealed that he had been abruptly yanked from bed. A crowd of curious Chandlerville residents collected near the car and peered at us with disapproving glances and unsympathetic remarks. They knew it was us that spoiled their fireworks and nearly set the town on fire. We were perceived no differently than the Frenchtown Gang. Our parents stood beside Lloyd Levin and the State Police troopers and held a private discussion. An occasional glance was made our way and Pa nodded several times during the meeting.

"Whad they do with yer stash?" Verdie asked Willie.

"I didn't tell 'um nothin'" Willie said in a hush while the blue statues stood near the cruiser with their shoes shining in the morning sun.

"You didn't tell 'um about the dynamite?" I asked, and we looked at each other with defeated surprise.

"Hell no."

"Them tricky sonzabitches. They told us they had you in the cruiser and we just figured you told 'um everything." Verdie said in total surprise. "Those bulls sure know how to get somethin' outta ya."

"They asked me a buncha questions, but I told 'um I was with yous guys last night and we just were hangin' 'round town waitin' for the fireworks ta start. They made me go with 'um here."

Collectively, we were no matches for the wits of the trained blue interrogators. They knew how to milk a group of kids of any information. We opened up like the floodgates of Kleber Dam spilling out what they were looking for.

"You still got it?" Verdie asked.

"Yeah, I've got mine stashed behind the old boiler down in the Ruins."

We pondered Willie's reply skeptically. The Ruins were not a good place to hide dynamite, there was a distinct possibility of it being found by others who made the Ruins their playground, "You gonna tell 'um where it is?" I asked.

"They probly' won't leave me alone until I do. Maybe they'll put me away for good if I don't." Willie said.

Main Street was collecting the usual morning traffic. They paused to gawk when they passed by. The troopers got inside the cruiser, and didn't speak as we drove away. We crouched as low as we could on the plastic seats trying to hide ourselves. Slowly and purposely we rolled past the onlookers on the streets. Like a scene from the old west, we were on display like a clutch of criminals being transported to the gallows.

The high arched ceiling at the entrance to the Court House echoed our footsteps when we walked across the chipped concrete down into the basement. The small jail room was dank with yellow walls that showed rust colored cracks where water seeped through. A narrow wooden desk sat in the corner next to the barred jail cell door. Quietly, and without hesitation we passed through the opening into the cell without instruction from the troopers who closed the steel gate with a 'clang'.

"The magistrate will be here in a while, but for now you boys will have to stay here."

The grey concrete floor was damp and worn from the pacing footsteps of past criminals. Vague initials and four letter words were carved into the plaster walls with omniscient epithets. It reminded me of the scribbling on walls of the shack on the Black. We took seats on the steel bench and sat with our heads in our hands, waiting to hear of our fate.

Outside the basement room we could hear the faint footsteps and mouthy whistle of Slim Wilkins. The door opened and he steered his galvanized bucket into the room with the mop handle. The fifty-five year old janitor, dressed in a one piece uniform with 'Trustee' printed in large black letters across his back, pushed the wheeled bucket of soapy water into the room and sloshed the mop head across the concrete floor. His bristling hair was white and receding to the middle of his head. He looked at us, and his sunken blue eyes looked bright and wise nestled deep in his whiskered face. He smiled as his flinty skin formed rows of wrinkles around his eyes. His red-veined bulbous nose showed his years of alcohol consumption but he was spry and light footed.

"So yous were the guys who blew up Chandlerville, ay?" And he chuckled. "If yas ask me, you should a started right here at the courthouse," he laughed displaying a row of rotting bottom teeth and a vacant upper gum. He tossed the dripping mop head onto the dusty floor in a splash and swished it around. "Yeah, spent a week a Sundays in that cell yer in, fellas. See those scratches on the wall above yas," he said pointing a bent finger toward the wall behind us where a collection of vertical gouges was carved marking his days spent there. The dozens of lines were crossed diagonally in sections of five. "Everything from fightin' ta disturbin' the peace." He paused with both hands holding the mop handle in front of him, "I'd have a few frosties and ride my old mare into the Northlund. That really pissed off Maggie, the owner. This was back in the early fifties. I used ta do it so often she had the doorway lowered sose' I couldn't ride in anymore." With a slap to his knee, and loud laugh, he continued, "Hell, I didn't let that stop me. I just got myself a Shetland pony and rode her in ta the bar."

"You use ta ride a horse into the Northlund?" I asked bemused.

"Yesiree," he grinned.

Our dour faces broken into smiles and we began to feel better. Slim set his mop aside and took a seat on the narrow wooden desk and began to tell us a story.

"Ya's see this uniform I'm wearin'? I get outta the county jail couple times a week to work in Chandlerville-community service they call it. I'm in ninety days for public drunkin'," he admitted with a defying snort. "Ain't like it was back in ol days. They'd jus' put ya in that cell and let ya sleep it off 'til mornin'. Anyway, gettin' back ta ridin' on ar' horses in the bar, well it all started back in Wyomin' when Benny McCain, P'air Lashuay, a Frenchman outta Canada, and I's ca'boyin' on a big ranch near Chugwater. We was best friends, and worked ar' tails off all week long movin' livestock ta high pastures in the summer and back down to lower ones in the fall. Then wez ride them horses in ta town and drink like fools in the bars. Hell, they didn't mind as much when we rode right inta the bar. They'd at least let us have a few before we had ta leave, got too crowded when everyone there was on horseback. One early fall, snow started in real soon and we still had some livestock pasturin' up on high ground, hunreds of 'um. Well, this ol boar Grissly got ta helpin' himself ta the white faces on a regular shift. He musta got a dozen 'er so. That ol' sombitch got ta where he'd jus' eat the guts outta the cows and leave the rest. Jus' broke their necks with one swat. One dark mornin' from ar camp, we hears this god awful fight goin' on. T'was that old boar and one na tha bulls havin' a death fight. By the time we got to 'um the Grisly killed the bull and ripped his throat out."

We pulled ourselves up to the cell bars, and sat on the damp floor with locked -in stares as Slim went on with the story.

"That's when Doc Moran, tha straw boss sent me, Benny and P'air out ta find that ol' bastard with ar' aught sixes. We packed enough grub fer a couple days ride cause it wunt gonna be easy findin' the maroddin' bastard. First day we tracked 'em fer miles in two foot a snow. Benny thought he caught glimpes of 'um when we rode into the timber line 'bout five miles outta camp."

Slim rolled up his sleeves, and deeply trenched scars showed across his forearms. He slid himself further back on the desktop. He paused for a moment and gazed toward the doorway in silence before continuing.

"We got ta the trees an' it were gettin' dark so we set up camp. Snow's comin' down in tons, an cold as an Eskimo's cock in the Klondike, it was. We was pretty high up in the wood plateau, and Benny an P'air went off ta find some quakies fer a campfire. I stayed ta set the tent. Christ, it were snowin' so hard by now ya couldn't see yer hand in front a yer face. I toll 'um ta take the aught sixes with 'em, but Benny said, 'Hell no, can't carry as much wood with a rifle strapped ta ma' sholder,' but P'air was packin' a .44 pistol, and they thought that was good enuf," Slim shook his head recalling what happened next. "Well, I hears this god aweful scream, it was P'air. That cocksukin' bear came at 'um like a freight train. It happen'd so fast P'air didn't have time to pull his Colt. Oh, I'll never ferget the screams and cries. When I got to 'um P'air was already dead-bear bit right through his neck and kilt 'em right now," Slim said with a snap of his fingers, "then he got hold a Benny. Benny was humped up in the snow all wrapped in a ball with the Grizzly just chompin' at 'em. I raised my rifle up but the snow had packed the scope. Tha bear saw me n' came chargin'. I held my arms up in front a tha sombitch but he chomp'd me real good on both arms, see..." he said revealing his mangled forearms. "P'air was dead, I could tell cause blud was poorin' outta his neck. Benny's back was broke but he managed to get the .44 and fired a shot. The 'ol boar turned toward him and that gave me jus' enough time to stick the rifle barrel to tha back a his head an' I kilt him with one shot."

    We sat closely together leaning against the cold steel bars of the jail cell in silence; imaging what horror it must have been to be in that scene. Our current troubles were nothing like Slim's encounter, his was life and death. Slim continued, "We was a real mess. Benny's back is broke, P'air's dead and I'm chewed up like an ol' dog bone. Took me two days ta drag us back on the horses ta camp-in a blizzard," he placed his cupped hand under his chin, "That's when Benny changed, he kept to himself-hardly talked ta no one. He blamed himself for P'air dieyun. He felt if he'd brought his rifle, P'air would still be alive. When he got outta the hospital he packed 'er up and came back ta Chandlerville...So did I, and I ain't seen nor spoke to 'um since."

    Slim rose from the desk and grabbed his mop. He chuckled when he looked at us lined up against the steel wall like kids in the front row of a theatre watching a scary movie. He slid the drenched mop head in front of us and mopped his way to the door. His bucket and faint footsteps crossed over the courthouse entrance quietly while he whistled his unfamiliar tune.

Chapter 22
The Clean Up

Up town, Lloyd Levin cleared a path in the crowd for the State Police Chevrolet panel wagon and it pulled quickly into the driveway next to the funeral home. The large crowd standing on the sidewalk and street was warned to move to the other side of the road. A pair of bomb experts dressed themselves in bulky jackets and helmets and marched through the doorway leading to the long stairs and climbed to the top in haste. Within a few moments they slowly exited, and walked to the panel wagon in short cautious steps carrying a metal box containing five sticks of dynamite wrapped in old newspapers. A short boxy expert removed his helmet and streams of sweat rolled down his forehead. His close cropped red hair shined in the morning sun like dew on a red lawn.

He addressed Romeo and Mildred Cosette, and the troopers standing next to them, "This stuff was at its most dangerous state.

The sticks were covered in white powder and that means it's extremely unstable. The slightest jolt could set it off. You don't know how lucky you were," he said brushing his temples with his leather glove.

"We've got to find out if there is any more dynamite," Trooper Riley said. "Trooper Moore and I will talk to the boys. Willie has been pretty tight-lipped so far, and I think he's holding back."

"Do you have any idea where he may be keeping it, if there is any more," he asked the Cosette's.

"Dem boys don't tell me nuttin'," Romeo Cosette said dismayingly, "Ask dare mudder, she'd know better den I would."

"They haven't said anything to me," Mildred replied.

"We'll find out," Trooper Moore said confidently, and the two blue troopers stepped inside their cruiser and drove toward the courthouse.

Chapter 23
Fish Tales

We sat on the steel bench that was the bed for incarcerated inmates like ourselves.

"You got that knife handy," I asked Verdie.

"Yeah and he pulled it from his pocket. I flipped it open and began to scratch a vertical line in the plaster below Slim's carvings to mark our first day in the slam. I signed below it: The Dregs.

"You think they'll really give us stale bread and water?" Denis asked recalling what Pa had told us about being locked up. "Stale bread 'n water is all dey give ya in da slammer," he often told us when he warned about getting into trouble.

We heard the trooper's steps approaching the basement door, and they entered. "Boys, we're going for a ride as soon as

Willie tells us where he put the dynamite." We were anxious to get released and Willie opened up like a tulip in the morning sun.

Willie led us through the shin-tangles and brush, and over the concrete abutments that encircled the old boiler. The troopers followed behind us, cautiously trying to keep the brush from soiling their impeccable uniforms. When we reached the rusted boiler, and Willie crawled under the far end on his hands and knees he turned to the troopers, "It's gone!"

"Look some more," Trooper Moore demanded with his hands wedged on his hips, "are you sure this is where you hid it?"

Willie searched further but found nothing. The cloth bag that contained the dynamite and fuse was nowhere to be found; someone had gotten to it before us. There should have been six sticks left over, we had used one of Verdie's six at the fireworks.

"Did you tell anyone where you hid the dynamite?" Trooper Riley asked the puzzled Willie.

"No sir, I didn't even tell those guys," and he looked our way.

All of us began searching the Ruins. We lay on our stomachs across the thorny raspberry bushes fervently pawing in all areas around the boiler. The troopers looked under a pile of rubble, Lloyd Levin turned over a chunk of broken concrete, but there was no dynamite. We fort members glanced toward one another suspiciously while thinking the same thing; what if Pratt got to it?

Finally, we backtracked through the snarled undergrowth with the police following behind, returning to the cruiser and another trip to the courthouse where Magistrate Crabtree was waiting.

His chambers were on the first floor beside the courtroom. We entered the hot, stuffy air of the wainscot and plaster room, and the spunky, grey-haired Crabtree looked small where he sat behind a sprawling wood desk. We would soon find out that like dynamite, explosive judges could come in small packages. He peered above his bifocal reading glasses and huffed, "sit down," and we took seats on the metal-framed chairs in front of his desk. We were really in for it. Crabtree was known around the county as 'the hangin' judge'. No guilty defendant had ever escaped his implacable anger and his stiff, harsh sentences.

Troopers Riley and Moore stood stiffly behind us and removed their hats. Riley spoke, "these are the boys that set off the dynamite last night at the fireworks, Magistrate Crabtree."

"Is that so, boys?" The spindly magistrate asked.

Verdie stole a quick glance my way, and I said, "yes, yer Honor."

The magistrate rose from his chair and leaned across the wide desktop, and looked at us above his glasses again. Like a shaken bottle of warm Coke, he burst out a barrage of verbal ass chewing like we had never heard before.

"You little sonzabitches, don't you know what could have happened? There could have been people killed last night!" He pounded his small fist on the desktop, "I should jail you cocksuckers for life for pulling that stunt."

We looked at each other with surprised and baffled faces fascinated with the foul-mouthed magistrate swearing like a sailor. He continued, "Where the hell did you come up with the dynamite, did you steal it?"

"We found it in a shack on the Black River, yer honor," Willie answered quickly.

On the wall behind the desk was displayed a large spiny-finned walleye mounted in a slightly rising curve with a crawler harness hanging from its toothy mouth. Next to it were photos in wooden frames showing the magistrate and his fishing buddies holding long stringers of fish. The room was sour and we needed a diversion; a quick thought came to mind and what I was about say would lead either to a hug or a hanging. In a risky gamble I spoke.

"Them's are some decent jacks and 'eyes," I blurted out in my best voice admiring the pike and walleye photos, "bet you had a hellova time landing that one." I said not thinking about the swear word I let out while looking at the longest pike on the stringer. I bit my lip and cringed waiting for his reply.

The judge raised his head and looked at me in utter surprise. The troopers' eyebrows rose when I swore, but the proud magistrate didn't care, "Why, thank you, yes they are," he smiled, "Caught this bunch up near White River, Ontario on the Little Kabe Lake," he boasted and pointed to the faded print, "those were caught on the Rainy in fifty-five," he pointed to another photo of him holding a mess of brook trout.

I had him by the balls of his swelling ego and massaged it for all I could, "Judge, you shoulda seen the lunkers Denis and ..." I stopped for a moment and refrained from naming Johnny, "...and I caught the day we got the dynamite. Right on the bend in front a the shack. Twelve pounder and a ten!"

Denis smiled and spread his hands far apart, "I caught the twelve, he caught the ten," he bragged; now permanently believing in my stretch of the truth, "fed us all for supper," he added.

Magistrate Crabtree relaxed his frown, and sat down on his chair in unveiled interest, "What did yous catch 'um on?"

"Red dare-devil, judge," Denis replied.

"I got the ten-pounder on a #9 with a gob a crawlers," I said remembering Johnny's rig.

"Pretty good hole was it?" He asked with serious interest.

"Oh, boy, we could a stood there and emptied the river. One right after another but we only took enough for supper." I said trying to prove how prudent we had been. Verdie and Willie relaxed in their chairs feeling the tension dispersing like a fish being removed from a lure.

"That's the ticket boys-take only what you need and leave the rest for someone else," the magistrate complimented.

Standing straight as string and somewhat bewildered, the blue troopers watched in amazement at my disarming conversation and how the magistrate succumbed to my buttery compliments. "A hum," Trooper Riley grunted to jog the magistrate's attention back to the dynamite.

Magistrate Crabtree tugged and repositioned his green and blue-striped tie, and let out a long breath, "Boys, what yous did was wrong. I can't believe you or someone else didn't get blown to pieces," he waited in silence, and looked at the troopers, and then he looked at us where we sat lamenting our behavior from the night before. "Here's what I'm going to do. You boys are sentenced to house confinement for two-weeks. No going up town unless your folks send you to the store but that's all. No further than your own backyard-two weeks, you hear?" He slapped his hand on his desktop, "take 'um away," he motioned to the troopers with a wave of his hand.

We rose from our seats, and the troopers lead us to the door. Magistrate Crabtree walked from his desk and put his hand on my shoulder, "When you're done with your punishment, what do you say yous boys take me to that old shack and we'll catch some of those jacks you talked about?"

"You can count on it, Judge," I replied. The blue troopers shook their heads in bewilderment and led us to their cruiser.

Trooper Moore leaned over the front seat and asked, "are you sure you boys don't know who may have taken the remaining dynamite?"

We looked at each and with our palms opened, "No idea, sir," Willie replied. We had a hunch, but there was no way of knowing at that moment. Regardless of how we felt about Pratt and the Frenchtown gang, we weren't going be ratfinks.

"If you hear anything about it or find out who took it call us," the trooper advised and handed Willie a blue business card with the State of Michigan seal embossed in the center.

"Will do, sir," we promised.

The cruiser pulled to the curb in front of the funeral home, and Pa and Mom were waiting in the full windowed lobby. They delivered us and the magistrate's sentence like parolees on work release, just like Slim Wilkins. What we didn't know was the troopers, Lloyd Levin and our parents thought a good scare from the fiery magistrate could shake us into walking the straight and narrow. It was all planned except for Crabtree's sentence.

"The magistrate said the boys have be confined to the house for two-weeks," Trooper Riley explained, "no further than the backyard, but if you need something at the store one of them can do errands, but only one at a time. This one here really sidetracked the magistrate. They got off pretty easy if you ask me," Riley added and pointed to me.

"Oh, I know; when he starts talkin' better hold on. If bullshit was music he'd be a brass band, but I got plans for da boys, believe me," Pa proclaimed in a stern tone, "dare's a lot of tings they'll be doin' 'round here." He reached over and pulled us together in a straight line like a teacher would do to misbehaving kids in class. "You hear 'dat? Yous go nowhere 'til I say so-two weeks," and he thanked the troopers.

"Remember what I said, boys," Trooper Moore said as he walked through the doorway, "you call us."

Pa looked at us suspiciously after he thought about the trooper's remark, "what he mean by dat?"

"Oh, they want us to draw a map to where the fishin's real good," I lied. We, certainly, didn't want to discuss the missing dynamite any further, especially with Pa.

Our work release began that afternoon with the old paint-peeling garage. Pa drove to Ellenberger's Lumber and Hardware where he bought an assortment of scrappers, brushes and a couple gallons of white paint. He opened the twin garage doors and removed a rickety wooden ladder and stood it up against the side of the garage.

"Dare," he said, "yous start here. I want it scrapped real good and when yous are done you get me an' I'll inspect it," and he retreated to the funeral home.

"Two-weeks," I said. "How we gonna get through this, it's the first day and I feel like a caged skunk."

"Ya know, we haven't practiced for a long time." Verdie reminded us about our bows and cattail arrows.

It was true; we hadn't shot a single arrow since June. The cattails we got down at Tuffs would be dried to perfection. We had a good bunch of them standing in the fort that hadn't been notched. The maple sapling bows were still strung and probably needed new strings.

"I'll run over in the mornin' and grab the stuff," Verdie said as he dragged his scrapper across the white curls of paint at one end of the garage.

The afternoon sun dragged across the sky heading for the western wall of clouds that were hanging like billowy puffs of smoke over Tower. Lenny Scully drove his flatbed truck loaded with coal into the alley and parked next to the coal shoot's trap door. Pa stepped from the side door of the embalming room and called us to help Scully unload the black hunks into the basement bin.

Lenny, 'Numb', as he was called, because of him being stupid and only fit for a laborers role in life, stood on the carbon mound holding a wide bladed shovel. He was incapable of anything that would require more than the use of his strong back and arms, and he never understood why he was called, 'Numb'. He was wearing a red and grey plaid shirt with frayed short sleeves that were unevenly severed by imperfect scissors. He looked down at us from his 'king of the castle' position and smirked, "That was quite a show last night, fellas. Really ruined the night. I saw it all from the top of elevator at the granary. We got the best seats in town from up there." And he laughed and turned his head away to spit tobacco juice in the alley, and a drip collected on his chin.

Chandlerville wasn't unlike any small town where 'news' travelled on the breath of gossip tellers. The coffee shop, the post office and the collection of farmers that met at Hopkins' Granary found out about crops and cattle, and kids with dynamite. Bored people embellished their blather to sound more interesting from the next guy's. Chandlerville was no exception; they thrived on it with their savory exaggerations.

Numb pushed the coal toward us with his shovel as we tossed the ebony pieces into the bin. He stopped and placed both hands on top of the shovel handle, "I just been wonderin', where did yous come up with it?" he waited for a reply and we kept silent, then he added insolently, "I know if yous was my kids you wouldn't be able to sit down for a week," and he resumed shoveling.

Denis' face transformed to a squinty frown and Verdie shook his head in disdain at the arrogant and meddling remark. I was insulted, too. I worried that Denis' temper would take over and he would start chucking coal at Numb Scully. If it was a story he wanted to take back to the morning gossipers, then I was going to give him a douzy.

"You really wanna know where we got it?" I asked with irreverence, and then I cautioned, "whatever you do, don't tell anybody, okay?'

Numb, with piqued interest, resumed his resting position on his shovel, "Won't tell a soul, I promise."

When he said, "I promise" I nearly broke into a laugh, but I remained poised and collected. Bill Pratt would become an altar boy before Numb Scully could keep his promise at the farmer's gossip meeting the next morning.

"Back in June, we was approached by the State Police. They heard that some guys in town were plannin' a bank heist at the Chandlerville State Bank. They told us they needed an undercover squad ta work with them to find out who's gonna pull it off. They were lookin' for some trustin' kids cause the bank robbers were some local hudlum's that lived down by Frenchtown, and they knew we was perfect for the job."

Numb's eyes widen and he wiped the spit from his chin, "I betcha it was that gaddamn Pratt gang. Ya know we caught him stealin' at the Granary, he's a sumbitch."

The bait was cast and the hook was set; I had him on the line like the jacks we caught on the Black. "You promise now, don't ya? This can't get out 'cause it would ruin the cops plan," I asked him while trying to keep a straight face.

"Oh, I won't tell a soul, like I said," he repeated his promise in a low whisper, and moved closer to me, kneeling uncomfortably on the jagged coal.

I turned my head from side to side glancing in each direction to make sure no one was within earshot other than us, like clandestine spies did in the movies, " Remember, you can't tell a soul what I'm about ta tell ya," and he nodded excitedly, "Trooper Riley and Trooper...what was that other trooper's name?" I asked my brothers.

"Moore, yeah, Moore," Verdie replied and Denis nodded following my lead.

I leaned in close to the flatbed and continued, "The troopers said they was gonna wait for this gang to break inta Ellenbergers' and get some dynamite to pull off the robbery. Ya see, Ray, Tom and Bobby was in on it, too. They was workin' with us under cover with the Troopers."

"Ya mean the Ellenbergers' is spies, too?" Numb said in awe. "I thought they was purdy quiet lately like they's holdin' sumpun' back," he reasoned; then he begged, "what happened next?"

"Okay, here's where it gets tricky," I said spinning out of control with the story. "The Ellenberger brothers wait for weeks and nothin' happens, so all of us meet behind the store and the trooper tell us that maybe it's too hard ta break inta the store. So we agree we'll go down there some night and break in through the sliders an steal some of tha dynamite like the robbers would do, ya know, make sure it's easy to break in an all. So one night we goes down there and gets a few sticks like the troopers and the Ellenbergers' want us ta do."

Numb leaned in with his tobacco face showing the intensity of a kid listening to a good bedtime story, "Don't tell me," he interrupted and proceeded to finish my story. "I betcha the troopers wanted yous to set one off where it was safe, like the fireworks where there was a fire truck and firefighters to control everything, and make sure the dynamite was gonna work okay, right?"

The power of suggestion is a wonderful tool when used in the presence of a moron. Numb Scully believed everything I concocted, and even provided an ending to the wild fairy-tale. I was delighted. I wasn't sure where I was going with the spin but he was able to conclude it nicely, even believably.

"That's why the troopers came to the funeral home this morning, and took us to Magistrate Crabtree… you know he's in on it, too," I added.

"I won't tell a soul; this is great," he gleefully added then asked, "ya think I can be in on it, too? I always thought I'd make a good spy."

We brothers looked at each other like we were considering a new member to the fort. We hesitated for a moment in thought, and Verdie and Denis in a 'what the hell-why not' shrug agreed. I remember the entrance exam. "The only way to do it is pass the 'can a teeth' test. We had to prove ourselves to the troopers, so you'd have to take the same test."

Numb looked down on us and considered my condition of entry, "I can pass any test 'at yous guys took, I can do it. What's tha 'can a teeth' test?"

Denis promptly ran to the embalming room and removed the New Era Potato Chips can and hurried back to the truck. Numb peered into the can and cringed at the mound of yellow dentures. I explained what to do. He turned his head toward the other side of the alley and flung the wad of Red Man from his mouth, and replaced it with a pair of stained false teeth.

"Zith ong euff," his muffled voice carried over the clumsy plates.

"Yer in," I proclaimed, and cautioned, "Remember, you can't tell a soul."

"I swear," he said while spitting out the remaining pieces of tobacco, and clearing his mouth of the bitter teeth taste.

He hopped in the cab and began to drive away sitting tall and proud.

"Ay," I cried out, and he turned his head back at me through the window opening. I issued a warning, "loose lips sink ships," and he replied with his thumb pointed skyward and drove down the alley carefully looking left and right checking out the backyards and houses where children played, like an undercover spy would do, on his way to the granary.

Denis fell to the ground and Verdie rolled on top of him in raucous, rambunctious laughter. I jumped on and they wrestled me to the bottom of the pile. In heaping adulation, they poked and prodded me with their stiff fingers and we rolled on our backs laughing so hard that tears welled in our eyes.

"Where in tha hell do ya come up with these stories?" Verdie asked in admiration.

"They jus' come...don't know where from, it just flows out," I humbly replied. I really didn't know, they just appeared in my mind as if I was watching a scene play out in a movie or on TV.

Chapter 24
The Warrior and The Saint

We finished painting the garage and Pa gave his approval. Then we were given the next chore of scrubbing the floor in the lobby, then the carpet in the chapel. Each task was completed, and we proceeded with the next one as our days of confinement streamed out in a continuous list of errands and assignments. Cleaning the embalming room was the worst job on our detailed list. There were blood splatters and chunky specs of who knows what clinging to the edge of the porcelain table. The red and black-checkered tile floor reappeared like a cleansed Phoenix as we scrubbed away the layers of crud around its base. Cobwebs hanging high in every corner were whisked away and empty Frankenmuth bottles that were inconspicuously hidden behind boxes of embalming fluid were tidied up for a possible 'flip' at Fassbinder's, even the New Era Potato Chips can was cleaned.

The days dragged out as slowly as a drifting sailboat trying to make way in a windless sea. The bronze bell that bonged at noon every day atop the courthouse peak was our way of counting down each day by Verdie reciting, "that's four days" and then "seven days" until we were near completion of our jail sentence. Outside a tempting sun rose and set every day above the warm wind begging and teasing us to return to the marching summer.

A lull in the lingering list of labors presented itself so Verdie sneaked over to the fort in the early morning sun and gathered a stack of arrows and our bows, propping them against the garage. A moldy bale of hay that had been sitting at the far end of the square yard since June was our cattail backstop. Denis took his bow and examined the string, "She'll be good for a couple shots," he remarked.

"Mine, too," Verdie said as he tugged the string on his and cradled a long cattail on his left fist that held the bow. He drew back and aimed carefully at the bale and let the cattail fly. The brown bloom on the end of the arrow struck the bale low to the ground missing his intended spot and puffed a cloud of white down. "Boy, rusty," he said reaching for another cattail.

There were two ways of using the cattail arrows; with their brown cigar shaped heads intact or cutoff. The heavier ended cattail was difficult to shoot over any distance, but was good for short-range shots for frogs and rabbits. But for a distant target we cut the bulbous ends off. Three split feathers for fletching were fastened near the nock with fish line and airplane glue. A couple of stolen plucks from Jack Newsted's objecting geese provided the feathers. Denis was a master cattail arrow fletcher, and was the best shot among us.

"Chris, get that old tire from tha back of tha garage," Denis said while cutting a notch where the cattail would fit on the bowstring.

"Got it," I said, and I tipped the tire to drain the stagnant water that had pooled inside. I knew what he wanted to do so I stood by the garage with the tire ready to roll across his path.

"Give it a go," Denis said and he pulled the six-foot arrow back on the binder twine string with a frowned concentration. I rolled the tire and he released his arrow. The heavy cattail sailed in a long arch across the yard and went through the middle of the rolling tire and struck the bale dead center.

"Good shot!" Verdie yelled.

"Another," Denis asked, and he knocked the cattail to his string with his face reflecting a more serious tone. This time he would use one that he had made with goose fletching and a sharply whittled end. "Put that empty can in front a tha bale," he asked but it sounded more like an order. I fetched the paint can. He took a deep breath, and drew the arrow back to the corner of his mouth, and held it in place for a long moment as he peered down the brown shaft with narrowed eyes. "Now," he commanded in focused attention. The tire looped toward the garage when I gave it a forceful push, and with William Tell like precision the arrow hurled through the tire's opening in a straight trajectory and pierced the paint can with a crunching 'thud', and lay splintered on the ground. Denis remained poised and stared at his target with a look of desperate determination like a soldier fighting on the front lines of some great battle. For a moment I was flabbergasted with his archery ability. He was the only one I knew who could pull off a shot like that. I looked at Verdie, and we both felt the chill of fear come over us. Masked behind Denis' affable smile and twisted cowlick lay a cold and calculating primordial hunter; for the first time I was afraid of him. I could see what he was capable of, and I pitied anyone who would evoke his cunning wrath.

"Ay," came the raspy sound of Froggy's voice from behind the fence. I peeked through the thin opening between the boards.

Craig, Willie, Lamb and Froggy were collected in boredom with their hands stuck deep in their pockets.

"Still in jail?" Willie laughed.

"Yeah, don't know if I can stan' it much longer," Verdie said leaning with one eyeball peering through the fence, "C'hup to?"

"Gonna check on the fort, maybe clean it up some," Willie replied while kicking the grass in Craig's yard, "feels like we're in jail, too," he lamented.

"How 'bout Pratt, run inta him?" I asked hoping they hadn't.

"Na, good thing, I'd kick his ass," Craig boasted and we chided him accordingly.

The upstairs porch window opened with the crunch of paint breaking away from the window jam for the first time since we painted it, and Mom looked down with surveying eyes where we stood huddled near the fence, "There's been a call and your father wants yous to go with him," she instructed, " come in an clean up." The exiled fort members painted themselves to the opposite side of the fence in a feeble attempt to hide from Mom.

"Oh, fellas," she quipped, "they got a few more days before they can join yous," and she closed the window.

Chapter 25
Onie

We pulled out of the alley in a wide turn stacked across the front seat of the long, blue hearse. Pa's Chesterfield smoldered in the dashboard ashtray until we passed the city limit sign where he retrieved it. We had become students of different smoking rituals. Pa's smoking routine was a quick flip of the top of his brass Zippo, a slide of his thumb against the flint's wheel, a long pull, a release of smoke blown down on his chest, then a wedge between an ash trays' notch until the next drag. Curly Bowman's style was more rigid but graceful. He skillfully constructed the handmade cigarette across his pinched thumb and index finger pouring the shredded tobacco from a cloth pouch into the paper crevice and twisting it into a perfect tube then dragging it across his wet lips to seal it. Fritz Krupp, on the other hand, would light his cigarette and never remove it from the corner of his mouth, and the spiraling smoke wafted past his heavy eyelids in a drifting grey column. When we had cigarettes we occasionally played the 'whose smoking now' challenge. One of us would carry out a smoking charade until another guessed who we were mimicking.

The gravel driveway we turned down meandered through a thick cedar swamp and rose to a green pasture of alfalfa on one side and corn on the other. Pa pulled the hearse next to an empty corncrib and backed it close to the steps of the porch. A litter of black kittens darted quickly behind their mother under a pair of weathered barn doors, and an old Blue Tick Hound rose from his resting spot in front of a tilting shed and staggered over to the hearse.

"Ay, old timer," Pa said to the inquisitive hound when he gave us a momentary sniff and returned to his resting place.

Gerhardt and Onie Radke's Michigan Farm house was in need of paint but the porch looked comfortable and inviting with two wooden armchairs nestled beside a square blue metal table that faced the neat barnyard. A pair of yesterday's coffee cups rested on top of a spread open Detroit News, testifying to the couples last evening together on the venerable porch. Onie had died during the night, and was still lying in their upstairs bed.

Pa gave the screen door a respectful knock and a young woman dressed in farmer's jeans, and an oversized blue cotton shirt opened the door. Her brown hair was pulled tightly to her head with a pinch clamp holding it together behind it. Her pale clay colored skin and reddened blue eyes revealed her anguish, but there remained a glow of handsomeness across her noble cheeks and lush eyelashes.

"Hi, Mister Cosette, I'm Delores… the daughter," and she offered her hand.

"I'm very sorry, Delores. We'll be a moment, den you can take us to yer mudder," and he returned to the hearse where we waited with the gurney.

Delores returned to the kitchen where her father sat with his elbows resting on the table, holding his sorrowful head in his weathered farmer's hands. Above the table an incandescent light bulb hung from the ceiling on braided electric wires and spread a yellow glow over the old man. A picture of the Last Supper hung on the opposite wall in a dusty wooden frame. A Seth Thomas clock ticked methodically on a dingy white wall and revealed eight-thirty while a pot of coffee began to perk on the stove. We steered the clumsy gurney past the screen door into the dining room.

"Mom's upstairs," the daughter said and pointed to a narrow stairwell.

A path was worn from the kitchen across the linoleum floor that lead to the stairs by decades of footsteps traveling in a certain routine. We approached the stairs with the gurney. The pine steps rose to a platform half way up and made a hard left to continue to an open ceiling bedroom. Verdie took the lead and Denis held the back end of the gurney, I followed. When they reached the platform the gurney was difficult to maneuver between the constricted plaster walls that had begun to separate and bow away from the lapboard. Verdie held the gurney firmly while Denis made several attempts to swing it in place to proceed up the stairs. Denis looked up at Verdie with a frustrated glance and they knew if they made the difficult turn how would they make the more difficult return with Onie Radke strapped on the gurney. We would have to improvise and worry about that when we descended the stairs.

The bedroom encompassed the entire upstairs. There was no bathroom or enclosed closet. A pair of single pane windows provided enough light for us to see. Dresses and work clothes hung on wooden hangers on a strong wooden dowel fastened to the roof rafters. An ornate oak vanity with dull brass handles sat against the wall and its mirror had faded edges. An opened jewelry box held a pearl necklace draped over its sides, and there was a photo propped in a silver frame of her wearing them at a wedding. A gold pendant, a pair of jade earrings and a brown marble handled hairbrush lay nearby atop the honey burled vanity top. A gold embroidered cushioned stool sat close by. On the wall near the bed, a photo of grandchildren snuggling near Onie Radke sitting by the Ocqueoq Falls portrayed a happier time.

I stepped closer to where Onie lay on her portion of the bed beneath the neatly spread bed sheet. Her long grey hair was combed and fashioned perfectly across her lacey pillowcase by the gentle hands of Gerhardt. Her face still held a fading rose-colored glint of life, but despite her natural appearance she was dead. Below us we could hear faint sobbing rising from the kitchen. Onie meant everything to Gerhardt Radke, she was the blood in his veins, the urge that made him take his next breath and the reason he rose from his bed every morning for the past fifty years.

We sat the gurney beside her and Denis and Verdie gently pulled her on. Wide canvas straps were cinched across her body to hold her in place. Pa came upstairs and stood watch and I kneeled by the gurney holding it in position. The four of us raised the collapsed carrier and its legs snapped into place with a series of clicks; we were ready for the intrusive descent down the tight stairwell.

The wheels of the gurney thumped over the pine floorboards as we slowly pushed it toward the stairwell. Again, the gurney legs were collapsed for easier handling. Pa went down the stairs ahead of us. Denis took the lead end of the gurney to the first step, and Verdie held the top end firmly above him. Onie lay quietly aboard. Despite Denis and Verdie's strength, Onie and the gurney, by force of gravity, took over midway down the stairs. Onie's thin corpse began to slip through the straps and slide toward

Denis. Suddenly, the force of the tilted gurney became too much for Denis to control and Verdie desperately clung to his end trying to prevent a free falling gurney. I grabbed at the back of Verdie's shirt trying to hold him in place but to no avail. Denis stumbled and fell to the landing; the gurney broke loose from Verdie's grip and followed, Onie Radke shot from her restraints like a sailor being buried at sea and landed in Denis' lap. I looked down from the top step at the wreckage below me behind a shocked gasp. Verdie now lay across the gurney in place of Onie; Denis cradled Onie in his lap like a child holding a porcelain doll. Then we devised a plan for crowd control.

Pa was in the kitchen consoling the Radkes, and the sound of the debacle miraculously didn't reach their ears. "Verdie," I whispered, "see if you can carry the gurney past Denis and set it up in the dining room."

"Ahhh, I think I can," Verdie said while hoisting the awkward gurney over Denis.

We were all breathing hard and I tried to shush them, "Denis, when Verdie's set up see if you can carry Mrs. Radke in your arms and set her on the gurney," and I stepped to the landing to help him rise and lift the body. As though he were Saint Christopher himself, Denis cradled the limp body across his folded arms and brought her to the upright gurney where we strapped her back in place. Pa and the Radkes sat below the yellow light and drank black coffee, never knowing what had happened.

The body was loaded in the long tunnel of the hearse. Outside the grey barn doors, the litter of black kittens sat comfortable beside their mother and studied us intently as we drove away. Perhaps they knew something that should never be told.

Chapter 26
The Death Notice

Denis and Craig loved fishing together. Craig's father often took them to the Black, The Rainy and the Little Canada out in the Jack Pine plains of Montmorency County. Phil Flynn doted over Craig and tried to spoil him with the newest fishing gear or a new bike but it didn't matter to Craig as long as he could go fishing with Denis. Being a member of the fort we wouldn't let him get spoiled. From a distance it was sometimes hard to tell the two of them apart, and the pair often confused people by their similar looks. Denis was sometimes called Craig, and Craig Denis. It bothered Craig that Denis and he were separated for nearly two weeks; they never went that long during the summer without some kind of fishing trip, either with Mr. Flynn or by themselves. One day remained on our sentence but Craig couldn't wait so he begged his father to talk to Pa to gain Denis' early release.

Phil Flynn entered the funeral home's lobby where Pa sat at his desk writing checks paying a pile of bills. The neat and clean pharmacist's white lab coat Flynn wore was in direct contrast to the bloodstained coat Pa wore in the embalming room. His short reddish hair was impeccably combed and shined from the Vitalis he palmed into it that morning. There was a confident cockiness in his manner as he delicately chewed a piece of spearmint gum while he spoke.

"Good morning, Romeo," he said politely. Denis and Craig sat excitedly on the stoop outside the lobby entranced with their fingers crossed hoping Craig's father could gain Denis' parole.

"'Mornin," Pa replied and set his pen on the desk, "how's da family, I don't see dem too much?" and Pa offered him a seat by his desk.

"Oh, everything is fine. June's been busy helping Carol get ready for college," he paused, "...and Craig, well, he's really havin' a hard time not being able to fish with Denis."

"Well, dey should be able to go in a couple days," Pa replied.

"Yes, I know, and I was wondering if I could have your permission to take him fishing today. I guess they've been doing well on the Black. I have lunches packed and I'd really appreciate you letting Denis join us today," he asked confidently.

Pa rested on his forearms against the desk and pondered the request. Denis and Craig kneeled outside the lobby door and peered through the window with begging eyes.

"Well, da boys have been workin' pretty hard. Maybe I can let him go," Pa said giving in to Mr. Flynn's request.

"Thanks a bunch," Flynn replied and shook Pa's hand. Denis and Craig, interpreting the conversation correctly through the glass, leaped to their feet and dashed off for their fishing gear.

Kleber Dam was their choice. They could fish above the dam from the sandy shoreline where the Black River paused in a sprawling pond waiting to be released through the concrete shoots, or below along the rocky river bank that rose and receded throughout the day when the turbines were engaged. The boys were familiar with the river, and they knew the very best fishing spot was on the two-foot wide concrete catwalk along the base of the three-story dam.

Phil Flynn parked his Rambler station wagon on the pit run stones that covered the parking area. A steep trail leading to the river was trenched into the clay and limestone where it ended at the river. The boys dropped the tailgate and began assembling their fishing poles while Phil Flynn hinged open a wooden lawn chair and began reading a book from a spot overlooking the river. A few anglers stood in the river and tossed blue fly lines across the chrome ripples with patient casts.

"Be careful down there, boys," Flynn admonished through an echo that bounced off the dam wall as the boys slid on their rumps down the steep path.

The boys stepped to the river's edge and set their rigs in haste. Denis plunged the sharp barbs of a blue-spooned crawler harness into a squirming Canadian Night Crawler and flung it across the shimmering water. The swift current quickly took the rig downstream then he reeled it back with steady turns of the Zebco's handle. Craig stood beside him and did the same. Cast after cast they tempted and taunted the brook trout, Northern Pike and pan fish with assorted lures where they thought the fish were laying. Nothing had taken their bait. Craig looked over to the frustrated Denis, "I know where they'll be bitin'," and Denis looked toward the threatening catwalk. They nodded in silent agreement.

The bronze water pooled calmly in a harmless eddy near the edge of the catwalk where they carefully stepped onto the wet wall.

The steel stringers they clamped to their belts dangled freely beside their legs as they inched along the narrow walkway to the middle of the river. High above the dam, thick strands of power lines converged and hummed monotonously at the top of several metal-framed towers that resembled giant erector sets. A foot below them the water now boiled threateningly in dark waveless swells around their feet. This was the place where the fish gathered and waited for tantalizing lures to dance before them.

Craig's first offering immediately produced a nice brook trout. Denis hoisted a furious small mouth shortly after. It seemed that anything they presented below the tumultuous water was ferociously attacked, and their stringers now hung heavily with fish against their wet blue jeans. They were casting into a sellers' market. They could sell anything to their aquatic customers. The stringers, now filled with fish and too heavy to hold on their belts, were snapped together and draped across the catwalk, but the boys continued to fish.

Sitting high above the river, Phil Flynn read his book under a bright sky but a cool breeze kept him comfortable as it drifted up from the cold Black River. No attention was paid to the rumbling turbines that began to awake within the dam. The dormant floodgates came alive releasing cascading blasts of turbulent water past the two boys where they stood on the perilous catwalk. Only when he heard the frantic screams of a fly fisherman did he know that something was terribly wrong. Far below, a single boy lay on his stomach across the drenched catwalk, beside the stringers of fish, desperately reaching and pawing into the raging water searching for his friend while the river exploded above him.

The same warm blue sky that drenched the Kleber Dam hung above the lazy afternoon in downtown Chandlerville. As though it were bundled and transported by a tattletale wind the news of a drowning reached the ears of the town folks. Rhiney Buza stepped from Leed's Grocery store with his bag of goods and walked toward his truck that was parked in front of the funeral home. Pa was taping Onie Radke's death notice against the lobby window when Buza entered and stood half way across the door's threshold. The phone schringed a couple times on Pa's desk and was answered on the upstairs extension.

"Hey, Cosette," he impolitely called, "I'm really sorry 'bout yer kid."

Pa turned to the ignorant messenger, confused and bewildered, "my kid?" he asked.

Rhiney Buza, in his most indelicate, insensitive and porcine manner blurted, "Yeah, didn't c'ha hear...he jus' drownt at the Kleber Dam!"

Romeo Cosette, the funeral director who consoled, caressed and comforted the mournful families of Chandlerville when called to duty now was stripped of his funeral director's armor; he was now a father receiving news of his son's death. He was crushed like brittle sandstone beneath the hammer of Rhiney Buza's heartless words. He fell back against the lobby window when his legs began to give out but he caught himself quickly. Buza, still standing smugly in the door opening, seemed to relish his position as the messenger of death.

A look of anger transformed the face of my father. In a raging charge he flew across the lobby toward the rugged Buza and grasped him by the throat with his trembling hands, "Vous ette un cochon terrible!" he screamed as Buza folded to his knees. Jeb and Janie LaFarge approached the funeral home window to discover where they would dine next and saw the two men struggling in the door opening. They intervened to diffuse the combatants. The struggle was over. Buza sat against the doorway beside his spilled groceries gasping for breath.

"I was just stoppin' in ta ask about the Cosette boy," Buza coughed and rubbed at the red marks left on his neck by my father's choke hold, "he jus went crazy!"

The LaFarges helped Buza to his feet and they departed the doorway while my father retreated to the long stairwell to deliver the devastating news to Mom.

Verdie and I were in our bedroom still restrained for one more day under court order.

We had heard the phone call but didn't know who it was from, or what it was about. The conversation and struggle that had taken place below us in the lobby was unheard, too.

Pa's slow and anguished climb to the crest of the stairs sounded unfamiliar to us and we wondered who it was. Each rising step he took brought him closer to where he would have to destroy hearts. He thought about fate and how it could be cruel. If Harley and Delores Maddox had driven to the hayfield and brought Timothy home instead of delivering his dinner, Timothy would still be alive. If he hadn't let Denis go fishing and remain grounded for one more day, Denis would still be alive. He thought about the consequences of telling Mildred Cosette her son was gone forever. Visions of every distraught mother's face he had seen at every funeral flashed through his mind like a horrifying hallucination. He entered the apartment and walked to the living room where he found Mom holding a rosary while a river of tears streamed down her warm cheeks. From our bedroom we could hear everything that was about to be said.

"Romeo," she said softly in a sad and delicate voice, "I just spoke to your brother, Jean," and her fingers fumbled on the beads of the rosary. "Jacques saw another vision of the Virgin Mary...."

Verdie and I rose from our beds and stood in the doorway and listened carefully. I recalled the conversation Pa had with Uncle Jacques when he was refused money. Pa sat down on the couch next to her and disregarded the strange news she just delivered, thinking of how he was going to tell her of something far more significant.

"Romeo, Jacques is dead," she said, and put her arms around him, "he drown himself in Saginaw Bay."

Pa leaned against the back of the green couch with his eyes closed and placed a trembling hand upon the rosary held by Mom. His eyes remained closed on his ashen face for an ephemeral eternity. He called us to the living room where we kneeled near them on the thin carpet.

Pa opened his eyes and his chest swelled with a deep breath, then he released the breath in three crushing words, "Denis is dead."

Chapter 27
The Resurrection

    The afternoon sun moved slowly toward its western target while apathetic people came and went about their business of everyday life along Main Street. Groceries were still being purchased at Leed's, postage stamps were still being licked and placed on letters at the post office, and Lila continued pouring coffee at the Midway. Life was sadly normal for every family living in Chandlerville, except for ours. An ocean of tears poured out through swollen eyes and fine memories of a son and brother turned in our minds like pages of a short novel that reached its end too quickly, and my father was reading two of them. I had never seen him cry before because he was strong, and a man's man. But even a man's man had his limit no matter how elastic he may be- eventually he would fray and collapse. In the still air of the tormented apartment, Mom lay in her bed on a tear soaked pillow inconsolable in spite of her rosaries' protective comfort. Verdie and I lay on our beds in silence with our faces turned to the walls refusing to look each other's way. We struggled to realize there would be no more spectacular cattail shots released by our warrior brother, no more ferocious glares of his quick temper, no more gulps of air drawn and released in his hilarious voice, and no more beautiful verse sung.

Intermittent calls rang from the yellow kitchen phone and were answered by Pa. Calls of condolences from caring people who had heard the news came throughout the late afternoon. Mrs. Dorsey delivered a heaping tray of sandwich meats and bread, and she asked to console Mom, but Pa had to tell her, "not right now". Soon the kitchen table was filled with trays of food dropped off by benevolent family friends. None of us were hungry.

Pa stepped into our bedroom, "you must come an eat something," and then he walked to his bedroom where Mom was.

We sat at the table without appetites and Mom appeared with Pa who steadied her with his arm around her waist. Her hair sprayed about her face in thick brown and grey strands, and her constant weeping had ceased, leaving her cheeks red and swollen. Salty tears had washed away the brightness from her blue eyes that had always danced warmly through her ever-present smile. In its place a lifeless gaze looked through us in an unfocused stare.

"Verdie, would you say grace?" Pa asked while helping Mom sit at the table.

Before Verdie could begin we heard the apartment door open and two blue troopers stood stoic and tall. In front of them, a boy with a cowlick in his hair, held a heavy stringer of fish; it was Denis.

Mom folded to the floor when she fainted and Pa's elastic wall shattered with a flood of tears. We gathered Mom and raced from the table to the miraculous scene. Mom and Pa fell to their knees and pulled the sobbing Denis in an embrace that took him to the floor. The blue statues of Riley and Moore stood at ease behind us and succumbed to the heartrending reunion and brushed away their tears. They waited respectfully before they spoke.

"There was a terrible mistake made today," Trooper Riley began, "because the boys look so much alike everyone thought it was Denis who drowned, but it was Craig."

"I tried to save him, Mom," Denis cried, "the floodgates opened and the water crashed on us. When we tried to get away he stepped on the stringer and fell head first inta the river... I tried ta save him," Denis was weeping uncontrollably now, "I had hold of his hand but the river jus' pulled him from me. I couldn't hold him anymore and he disappeared. I jus' couldn't hold onto him... I could see his face below the water and he was so scared an," in a final flush of tears, "...I tried to save him."

Denis rested his head against Mom's mollifying bosom and prayed, "Please forgive me, God."

Chapter 28
The Metamorphosis

The Flynn's apartment above the pharmacy changed from a happy home to a sterile, occupied house after Craig's death. Like a black blanket shrouding over it, darkness befell their family, especially Phil Flynn. His heart was slowly hardening like molten iron cooling in an impenetrable casting. His brash confidence withered from his bright face like green leaves left to brown on a felled oak tree. He was besieged with grief. He blamed himself. If only he had been more strict and careful where the boys fished. If only he taken them to another fishing hole. 'Ifs' would haunt him for the rest of his life.

Members of our fort served as pallbearers. We looked upon Craig for the last time when Pa closed the lid on the white casket. We lined up on each side of Craig's casket holding the cold handles as tightly as we could. It was difficult carrying our friend across the dried, crusty grass at Elmwood Cemetery to place him on the canvas straps of the lowering device.

Reverend Berger stood at the head of the casket, and the Flynn's sat dutifully on foldout chairs at the graveside. A funeral crowd stood unobtrusively about the other gravesites surrounding Craig's clutching damp handkerchiefs and prayer books. The Reverend recited a Mary Frye poem:

> "Do not stand at my grave and weep
> I am not there; I do not sleep.
> I am a thousand winds that blow,
> I am the diamond's glint on snow,
> I am the sun on ripened grain,
> I am the gentle autumn rain.
> When you awaken in the morning's hush,
> I am the swift uplifting rush
> Of quiet birds in circled flight.
> I am the soft star that shines at night.
> Do not stand at my grave and cry,
> I am not there; I did not die."

A funeral luncheon was held at the Lutheran Church. Family friends passed by the Flynn's table carrying plates of food and informal condolences; even a malignant apology from the LaFarges.

Verdie and I went to the funeral home's chapel and began our dutiful clean up. We relieved Denis from the chore, and he went upstairs. When we finished putting chairs away and swept up we joined him in our bedroom. Denis was sitting with his arms crossed atop the sill of the window gazing into the Flynn's apartment. Gone was the inharmonic sound of fingers misplaced on the piano keyboard, gone were the window conversations of hushed plans and schemes. We let him be in his emptiness.

Denis began to change. He never spoke of his last moment with Craig. Only Father Dudek, the visiting priest from Calcite City would hear of that day in a quiet confessional. The quick smile and clownish behavior succumbed to a sometimes-distant stare, and he refused to go to the fort. His tolerance for a practical joke was fading so we had to be careful what we said for fear of invoking his anger. He began practicing more with his bow, and spent long hours hunting by himself in Snyder's swamp west of town. In a frightening metamorphosis, a hunter warrior was now emerging.

Chapter 29
The War

Two weeks of solace drifted by in a staid doldrum of indifference as we moped about the protective apartment. Finally, Willie, and the rest of the fort members marched up the long stairs to our apartment. Mom let them in with a happy greeting. She knew we needed to return to the group in what she called 'the healing process'.

They entered the bedroom where Verdie was combing through pages of a science magazine. I was scripting naughty thoughts while looking at pictures of naked South American Indians in a National Geographic Magazine. Denis was helping Pa embalm a body, something he now seemed to gravitate to.

"Man, what tha hell is this," Willie said in an intolerant voice, "It's beautiful outside and yous are holed up here like a couple a bandits hidin' from Judge Crabtree."

We put our magazines down, and Verdie replied, "been kinda hard ta think about doin' stuff," then he revealed a concern, "I don't know 'bout Denis....He's been strange lately. He comes and goes without invitun' us... Goes off huntin' like a wild Indian. I'm kinda worried 'bout him."

Johnny and Froggy took seats next to Verdie. Lamb sat below me on Denis' bed.

"We haven't even gone to tha fort since it happened," Johnny admitted.

"Denis won't go," I said.

"That's gotta change, man," Willie claimed, "I say we head over there right now."

We gathered up like the posse we had always been and headed for the fort. Denis remained in the embalming room.

We fought through the new growth of weeds that had taken over the once trodden trail that led to the fort. As we approached we began to see that something was different. We stood at the entrance and beheld a scene that had worried us all summer; the fort had been destroyed. The wood planks that had made the roof were now dismembered and were tossed about in a wrecked pile. The stove was destroyed, and was half buried in rubble. Someone had demolished our haven, our sanctuary, and our home away from home. A piece of paper with the scribbling of misspelled words was impaled on a spike in one of the boards, it read:

WE NO YU TUUK AR DINAMIT WE WAN IT BACK ER ELS

"Pratt!" Verdie screamed, and he kicked at the caved in fortress in anger. Our suspicions were correct; Pratt had gotten to the dynamite but somehow had lost it. Now he blamed us.

We took knees to the ground and gazed at the heap of wood and earth that once was our fort. In the distance we saw Denis making his way toward us with his bow strapped to his shoulders and holding a fist full of cattail arrows. He stepped close to us and looked down at the remains of the fort. His face tightened and we waited for his reaction.

"It's time for war," he proclaimed through his clenched teeth. He was back, a true fort member wanting revenge.

We rose to our feet and beheld Denis with warm embraces and welcome back praises, and, as though from awaking from a ghoulish nightmare a familiar smile returned below the twisted cowlick on his head.

We sat in a circle near the fort planning the battle. We still had a hoard of cattails stacked in the garage. Our papier mâché helmets were retrievable beneath the rubble and we collected them by our sides. Willie and Verdie began strategies of what if's and where at's.

From the tall weeds behind the fallen fort we heard a stir and a voice called out in a low diluted tone, "Guys," the humble voice spoke out. The voice stood up and it was Dave Manton. His left eye was swollen and he was missing a front tooth. "Can I talk with yous for a minute, it's important."

We got to our feet in a defiant pose, and I asked, "Whadiya want, Manton?"

"Ya here lookin' for trouble?" Willie challenged.

Manton approached subserviently like a dog wanting to join a pack. "I gotta warn yous... Pratt's gonna attack anytime now," then he added in grave caution, "...and he's got reinforcements."

We pondered the information with suspicion, and Denis spoke, "Tell us more."

Manton joined us, we took knees to the ground again, and listened to the exiled gang castaway tell his story.

"Pratt has some cousins that came up from Flint. They're mean sonszabitches just like Bill. There's four of um. One named Scud, he's fifteen. Another called Barker cause he's always barkin' like a mean dog, he's sixteen and then there's the seventeen year-old twins, Hanibal and Canibal; those two are crazy!" he warned. "Pratt destroyed yer fort 'cause he thinks yous took the dynamite he stold under the boiler."

"That's ar dynamite, goddamit!" Will shouted.

"I know, he seen you put it there. And that's not all," Manton looked left and right from the corners of his eyes, "he's been braggin' he made Clifford Krupp fall from the Ruins."

A hush fell over our group as we tried to absorb Manton's revelations. Pratt was not only a bully, and a thief; his treacheries led to Clifford Krupp's death.

"Why you tellin' us this stuff, Dave?" Verdie asked solemnly.

Manton lifted his chin for us to see his face better, and pulled back the collar of his white shirt revealing fresh bruises and cigarette burns left by Pratt, and his cousins. They had ganged up on him when he told Pratt he was leaving their group.

Our faces sank in despair with the abominable news. Lamb began counting out a villain's roll call, "Pratt, Millender, O'Toole, that's three. Scud, Barker, and the twins, that's seven... Holly, shit!"

Denis sat quietly and listened. His eyes squinted in pensive planning; there was no sign of fear anywhere on his face.

I was perplexed; I didn't understand how Manton had become a part of the Frenchtown gang. How he could be an altar boy one day and the next fall so far from grace, like the Archangel Lucifer tempted and convinced him with some evil promise. I asked him and he answered.

"Yer an altar boy, aren't you?" He replied after a thoughtful pause, "all three of yous ar altar boys, ay?" And he looked at us brothers.

"Yeah," Verdie replied.

"Has he tried to do anything to yous, yet?" Manton asked with his head lowered.

"Whadya mean, like swear at us?" Denis asked.

I could see his eyes moisten, and he opened up while trying to hold back his tears.

"After my sister drowned, he started comin' 'round. Takin' me for rides, lettin' me drive, givin' me money, and gettin' real friendly," he held back for a moment, and his stifled tears began to flow. "He started doin' terrible things to me. Made me watch movies of people screwin' and suckin'." He looked straight into our eyes and admitted, "He forced me to let him suck me."

He wiped away the tears, and continued with a warning, "Stay away from him, guys. He's the devil!"

We remained sitting in front of the ruined fort for a long time. Not talking, just thinking. What was happening to our town, our lives? Our fort was in ruins, friends and family had died; one was murdered, and now we were about to face off against the bloodthirsty gang from Frenchtown.

Denis, sensing our apprehension and fear rose to his feet and addressed the group in a fierce conclusion, "There's gonna be a battle. You've got ta get that straight in yer heads. If we go inta it like scared rabbits then we'll never survive, they'll beat us to a pulp...maybe worse." He walked around us in a circle holding his bow like it was his best friend, "We can do this, but we got to be strong, don't show um no fear," he said and gripped his bow tightly in his strong fist.

Verdie looked up at Denis and stood beside him, "Fuckin' Ay! They want a fight so let's give um one!" he shouted. We all rose to our feet and let out defiant clamors of bravado and danced with our fists raised in the air and against our puffed out chests. We were ready.

Before leaving, Manton said, "Pratt's down in the Grove right now."

We chose to go on attack. The helmets were dusted off and the eyeholes were made perfect. Bows were restrung with fresh binder twine, and the best cattail arrows were collected, then we set out for Main Street.

We knew Pratt would surface somewhere up town causing some kind of trouble. With bows in hand, helmets in place and God on our side we marched ahead like a Roman Legion going into battle.

We stomped through the tall weeds like pissed off soldiers, departing the field and broken fort in unison. Maxon Field lay in front of us and we followed the fence line along the visitor's dugout. We marched up the alley between the Metropole and the Library and entered Main Street. We halted in front of the

Metropole under a seething sun, and the sound of Rah Madden's guitar and singing carried out into the street.

"We'll just wait here for a while, he'll be by," Willie said in a patient tone.

We looked to the east where the lazy, blissful street showed no sign of Pratt. Cars and trucks zoomed by in each direction, and the bell from the courthouse rang twelve noon. Suddenly, like Willie had become a visionary, and the clock was an aberration from a mystical boxing ring, we heard the raucous bellowing of the Frenchtown gang slithering up the street, coming from the Grove, all seven of them. Pratt was in the lead. They saw us and ran to within a stone's throw away from us. We bristled in anticipation, and they clenched their defiant fists and stood side-by-side facing us.

"Lamb, I want you to leave!" I shouted, and Verdie and Willie shouted at him in agreement. This was going to be too much for the smaller warrior. He wasn't of frame nor size to tangle with the vicious gang.

"No, I'm gonna stay," he screamed back.

"I said leave now!" I screamed again, and gave him a hard shove.

"Go on, Lamb, get outa here right now!" Willie yelled behind me.

Lamb flung his helmet to the ground and ran off in a dejected trot and never looked back.

An old Buick braked to a screeching stop in the middle of the street next to the Frenchtown gang. A short, burly man with a scrubby beard stumbled out of the driver's seat grasping a heavy metal chain; drunk, disheveled and wanting to fight. He swung the chain in menacing circles and cast a threatening glare at us. Ivan Pratt lined up next to his evil son. He looked at us, then turned to his son, Bill, "got cher self a rumble goin' on here, do ya? Think I'll have some fun with yous," and they began slinking toward us.

By this time the town took notice. People began gathering on the street, cars stopped short of the spot where we faced off and watched with great anticipation. A forty-nine Plymouth slid to stop at the curb; it was Chubba Harkins and Farny McIntosh. They jumped from the car and lined up beside us.

"Ya...ya...yous need a hand?" Farny asked, flinging his cigarette to the street.

"Jawny, I got cha cov' 'ud," Chubba said to Johnny.

Then it began.

Bill Pratt rushed up to Willie and struck him with his right fist and Willie fell to the ground. Verdie stepped over to Pratt, and landed a hard first on the side of his head. The dazed Pratt fell to one knee, Verdie proceeded to pummel Pratt's face and body with a wild barrage of punches.

Before I knew it, O'Toole had me in a headlock and we wrestled to the ground. O'Toole was stronger than I was and he gained the upper hand. He sat across my chest besieging me with a flurry of his fists that left me seeing stars. In one swift kick, Denis knocked O'Toole from my chest, and he folded to the ground. Then the crazy twins entered the battle and grabbed Denis by his arms. Froggy leaped in and dragged Cannibal to the street and they hurled fists upon each other in a frightful battle. Denis was able to regain his footing and Hannibal was no match for the raging wrath my brother set forth upon him.

Now it was Johnny and Millender. In a fighter's stance, they faced off against each other, each waiting for an opening to throw their punches. Johnny's landed first with a hard right cross that rocked Millender's head back, but Millender shook it off and delivered his own in return. O'Toole stood up, so did I, and we faced each other. In my wobbly daze I remembered the lesson Booz Danker gave me, and I darted in close to the raised fists of O'Toole, and pulled his body to my chest. I pressed my head against his eyebrows with all the strength I could muster. I felt the warm wetness of his blood spewing from his forehead down my cheek, and then I began throwing circular punches against his open back. Each fist landed on his kidneys with a sharp thud, and he let out an agonizing grunt. I grinded and punched until I felt his legs give way so I let him fall to the street writhing in pain.

Barker entered the battle. He sneaked up behind Johnny, and growled and snarled like a wild dog. Just when he was going to throw a sucker's punch to the back of Johnny's head, Chubba rushed up in a couple of leaping steps and blasted Barker's so hard that a loud 'crack' rang out. Barker lay at Chubba's feet like an obedient cur.

Ivan Pratt walked slowly toward the battle swinging his chain violently above his head. He was going to hurt someone. Rah Madden's music had stopped, and I heard the door of the Metropole open. I saw the bronze face, and brazen fists of Booz Danker glide across the sidewalk like a graceful dancer onto Main Street where he transformed into a majestic fighter's stance to face Ivan Pratt.

Danker's face took on a look of a professional; a look we had never seen before. There was no sign of a drunken stager, no wistful laugh, only the look of fighter in the ring.

Pratt approached the fighter, and laughed, "Yer a has been, you ole bastard. Better get outta my way," and he swung the chain faster above his head. Booz began bobbing up and down on nimble toes and his head swayed back and forth in a composed fighter's routine. Pratt rushed up and cast the chain toward Boozes head. Booz leaned to one side and came up with a crashing right hand to Ivan Pratt's face. Then he stepped back, and threw a left hook, then a right cross to Pratt's chin. Pratt fell to ground knocked out cold. Booz kneeled beside the dispatched Pratt and counted, "One... two... eight... Yer out!" He screamed, but didn't laugh. Danker looked around the hectic scene to see if any other Frenchtown gang members wanted some of him, but there were no takers.

    Bill Pratt, now collected and recovered from the ass beating he got from Verdie, stood up and pulled his knife from his pocket and flipped it open. Verdie was standing with his back to Pratt. Pratt raised the knife to plunge it into Verdie's back. The whistle of the cattail arrow shooting past my face was so fast and instantaneous that I didn't know what it was. The warrior's aim was perfect and Pratt fell to the pavement gasping for breath while clutching the cattail arrow that skewered his throat. A pool of blood streamed down his clothes and gathered around him where he kneeled, like he was an altar boy praying. The battle was now over.

Chapter 30
The Symbol of Chandlerville

Bill Pratt didn't die that day. He recovered, and fled Chandlerville like a thief in the night. So did his maniacal father and incorrigible cousins seeking the safer anonymity of Flint. There would be more space for evil deeds in the big city, and the Pratts' would explore every opportunity that presented itself.

We gathered in the safety of our bedrooms that evening no worse for the wear. Our bloody noses, swollen eye sockets and reddened cheeks bore testimony to a great battle waged earlier that day. Willie and the other fort members came by and we talked of our great victory.

The absence of Lamb concerned us. We had turned our backs on him, in spite of his bravery and willingness to fight. We, still, thought it was the right thing to do. He would have been destroyed, and we could never forgive ourselves. Sadly, we had broken our rule of honor by banishing him from the fight, and it destroyed our smallest fort member's trust.

The yellow phone rang, and it was another call. Pa climbed the stairs in his familiar shuffle, and arrived at our room to take us away to another broken family. Strangely, Pa asked for Verdie and Denis to accompany him, and I was left at home. Perhaps it was the lack of room in the front seat of the hearse because we had each grown over the long summer; perhaps it was for some other reason. I didn't mind staying at home.

The hearse pulled away, and I knew there would be a Chesterfield smoldering in the ashtray until they reached the city limit sign where Pa's next puff would come.

Another phone call and Mom answered. From my bedroom I heard Mom answer with 'I don't knows', and "I haven't seen him". The phone was put back into its cradle, and Mom came to my room.

"Have you seen Lamb Cavanaugh today?" she asked.

"He was uptown with us for a while, but he went home, why?"

"His mother just called and is worried; she hasn't seen him since this morning,"

I looked at her with puzzled eyes, and thought for a moment about the strangeness of him not going home. I began to worry.

"Not sure where he could be, Mom."

I hurried my feet into my tennis shoes, and bolted down the long stairs, and onto the sidewalk. A small gathering of people chatted in front of Leed's, and I walked up to listen in. I thought it strange that their conversation consisted of pointed fingers, and outstretched arms aimed toward the west end of town. Bob Leed spoke, "some little kid's stranded on top of the Ruins, someone just said. What the hell would some kid be doin' up there?" he questioned. The other participants agreed.

"Aw, that's got ta be a bad rumor, how tha hell could some kid climb up there?"

I knew immediately who it was they were talking about. It was Lamb.

I ran as fast as I could toward the Grove and the thick trail that led to the Ruins. The brush and branches slid over my chest and face as I rushed toward the tallest walls. A quick snap of a willow branch slapped me in the face with a harsh sting, but I pushed on.

I reached the rusted boiler and looked up toward the high crest of the four walls, the walls that held the faded red shirt. There was Lamb laying across the top of the narrow concrete; frozen stiffly in fright.

"What ar' ya doin'," I yelled up to him with the walls repeating my words in a harsh echo.

"Yous guys kicked me out a tha fort. I wanted to fight, but yous kicked me out," he cried.

He was frightened to his bones. He climbed the wall but after reaching the top he froze in fear. He looked down to the dark water, and held the wall tighter in his clutch.

"I wanted to prove to yous I wasn't afraid. I wanted to get the red shirt, and show yous," he revealed.

I bent down and tightened the laces of my tennis shoes, and began my ascent along the hard wall grabbing and holding onto the steel reinforcement rods.

"Don't move, Lamb. I'll be right there," I yelled as I slowly climbed toward him.

"Hurry, Chris, I'm scared," he agonized.

Lamb had made his way across the narrow surface and was nearly below the red shirt. I hoisted my leg over the shelf and sat next to him trying to catch my breath. A smattering of curious people had assembled below us and shouted well-meaning instruction our way. I was now between Lamb and the shirt. He reached over to me, and I took his hand firmly attempting to comfort him.

"What ar we gonna do," he gasped, "How we gonna get down?" he cried.

There it was, directly over my head, but hanging high on the hard to reach steel bar.

Lamb sensing my overwhelming curiosity looked at me through his bulging eyes, "don't do it," he pleaded.

I looked up at the shirt where it sat undisturbed for the past eight years. I looked at Lamb where he clung to the wall like a cackle burr on sheep dog.

Temptation is powerful. I paused and pondered what I was going to do next. I was responsible for Lamb Cavanaugh, now. I was there beside him, and he looked to me for his salvation. I was, also, beside the greatest prize Chandlerville had to offer; the red shirt.

The allure of the shirt overwhelmed me. I rose to my feet. I held my arms away from my sides. I reached for the shirt, and grabbed it. I grabbed the red shirt!

Far below people gathered like sad sheep in a barnyard. The crowd looked upon me with dumbfounded disappointment. I looked at them, and saw displeasure in their eyes. It was as though they didn't want the shirt to be removed. The shirt had become a symbol to the town, a challenge of will, a hope to succeed, a goal to strive for. If I removed the shirt all hope would be gone; Chandlerville would be robbed of every kid's dream.

I held the shirt in my hands for a short moment realizing how important it had become to the community. I reached high and placed it back on the steel bar. The onlookers sighed in quiet relief.

The blue troopers and Lloyd Levin stood below us now. A larger crowd had gathered.

Trooper Riley scaled the hard wall with a safety harness and fetched us like stranded bear cubs in a tree. There was no applause when we landed, no autographs or photos taken to mark my place in Chandlerville history.

The crowd began to disperse through the tangle of the Ruins. When we reached the police cruiser there was a cotton bag sitting on the ground by the driver's door. The very same bag Willie had put the dynamite in. Inside the bag a crumpled note read:

'Don't look for the dynamite- it's been destroyed'

Through the distant brush and shin tangles a bent figure made his way out of the Ruins, and disappeared like a fading rain cloud. It was Benny McCain on his way to find more treasures to hide or sell.

Chapter 31
The Last Page of Summer

We began the reconstruction of our fort during the waning weeks of August under fleeting summer skies. September mornings began with a cooler kick. The maple and birch trees that were so prevalent around Chandlerville began to show their age with muted brown and golden spots; like the colors that gather on the faces and hands of old folks.

Phil Flynn shrunk from showing any friendliness to our family after Craig died, darting into his store whenever he saw us coming up the street, and ignoring my father's hellos. It was as though he resented us because Craig had died and Denis had lived, but we understood. Carol Flynn went off to college, and Mrs. Flynn always gave Denis a sad smile. Perhaps, he still reminded her of Craig. But, an icy wall had formed between the two buildings where we lived, eventually melting away when the pharmacy burned down that fall, and the Flynns' moved.

Father Klein, mysteriously and without notice, was swept away by the shielding cloak of the church to carry on in some unsuspecting town in upstate New York. Benny McCain continued with his bent over travels throughout the ditches and back alleys on his quest for treasures. Booz Danker was never looked at in the same regard as before, even with his staggered walk down Main Street. But nothing else really changed. The red shirt still sat high above the walls of the Ruins, tempting and teasing the imagination of the young boys of Chandlerville, but not ours.

That summer was a dream. It was a dream inside a fairy tale where boys lived like heroes, and villains were dispatched into the gutter of defeat. Fish were caught, girls were kissed, songs were sung, and a friend was buried. But each of us grew into something greater, stronger and, perhaps strangely, content with being the Dregs of Presque Isle.

Amidst a sooner sunset and later sunrise, we tried to hold on to summer as hard as we could, but it slipped away just as Craig did in the raging waters of Kleber Dam.

Like a dream that could only be recalled, but not repeated, the summer of '63 was gone forever.

Decent!

Christopher Chagnon

Christopher Chagnon was born in Bad Axe, Michigan February 19, 1951; the seventh child of a family of twelve. He moved with his parents, Rollin and Mildred Chagnon to Onaway, Michigan in 1955 where his father, a funeral director, opened the Chagnon Funeral Home.

At an early age his mother encouraged him to read from the family's extensive library containing the works of Guy De Maupassant, Anton Chekhov, Mark Twain and Ernest Hemingway. But it wasn't until 1969 when Robert Donia, his high school English teacher, encouraged Chagnon to become a writer. While growing up in the rural northern Michigan town of Onaway, Chagnon was surrounded by a mix of interesting, indelible characters that have fueled his stories with rich dialogue and unforgettable scenes. But Chagnon's path first led him to becoming a photographer gaining prominence while living in Detroit. In 1976, he was hired by the

Detroit Tigers, and spent more than ten years as their team's photographer. He has spent time as the Detroit Pistons team photographer, photographer for the Associated Press, United Press International, hotel photographer for Detroit's Renaissance Center, and his photos have appeared numerous times in national publications. Throughout the '70s Chagnon wrote magazine articles, and newspaper features and he eventually opened a professional photo lab near Detroit.

Chagnon has three children, Justine, Marcel and Luc, and has moved back to Onaway, Michigan with his wife, Nannette, whom he has been married to for forty-two years. He is a full-time writer now and has had three short stories published. His first novel; 'The Dregs of Presque Isle', is the first in a trilogy, "The Chandlerville Chronicles".

www.ChristopherChagnon.com

The Ghosts of Presque Isle
Book Two of the Chandlerville Chronicles

The water swirled around my legs in tight circles as I waded further into the river. I feared the cold saturating current but kept going as the striped shirt boy nodded and continued to smile. I was up to my waist and the cold numbness I expected didn't come. I couldn't feel the river bottom. As though a trap door opened, and a strong hand had pulled at me, I fell into the depths of the bottomless river. I held my breath until my lungs were bursting. I pulled myself to the surface where the river was raging and tried to breathe, but there was no air. I was going to drown above the water. The hand pulled at me again and the river took me below. My body lay suspended in the rust colored water like a fly stuck in a spider's web. There became an umbilical like connection between the river and me. I didn't have to breathe anymore. Then came the smothering darkness. Darkness like I have never known. More gray than black, it surrounded me in a colorless, tasteless blanket of oblivion. A young girl appeared. Her long blond hair suspended about her delicate face where a sad scar was etched across her right cheek like someone had branded her. We were both caught in a translucent vacuum of an unknown space. Space where it was quiet and peaceful. She took me by the hand and we rushed through the grayness below the other world above us that was devoid of oxygen.

    I wasn't afraid anymore. But soon I saw the world above me raging in a violent storm. There was a great iron beast waging battle with the ruler of the other world. Desperate men clung to her broken belly like horrified children do to their mothers. Some of their bodies fell into my underwater realm and disappeared below me. We sped past the mayhem like a submerged missile and the grayness encompassed us again. We travelled into another place where there were stone walls built in a circle that held us in a stagnant jail. I knew this place; we were in the basement cistern. Her delicate face and gently floating, blonde hair that once was at home in the other world began to transform. Her fragile skin started to peel from her bones revealing a tawny skeleton, like the decrepit remains of Larry Burgess who was found weeks after he drown in Black Lake. She held my hand in desperation, not wanting to let go but I fought to break away. We were both drowning in the mire of the stonewalled cistern.

Expected Release: Winter 2013
www.GreyWolfePublishing.com

Made in the USA
Charleston, SC
21 November 2013